GREETING CARDS FOR EXES

Rebekah L. Purdy

*Warning: Not intended for persons under the age of 18. May contain coarse language and mature content that may disturb some readers. Reader discretion advised.

Cover Art Design by: Kelly Moran/Rowan Prose Publishing

Photo Credit: Adobe Images

First Printing

ISBN: 9781961967441

Rowan Prose Publishing, LLC: Peridot Imprint

www.RowanProsePublishing.com

Published in the United States of America

Praise for Rebekah L. Purdy

"Fun, low-stress read—kind of like ice cream on a summer day."
– HCNG Library

"A fun and flirty light read. Just what I was looking for."
– Flirtatiously Fictitious Reads

"Purdy presents a beautifully complex array of characters that touch your heart."
– A Bookish Escape

"Lots of duplicity, surprises, and twists in the story, but this reader was just unable to put the book down."
– Talking Books

"I was not able to tear myself away from this novel and barely gave anyone the time of day. Purdy has a very beautiful way of writing and describing the world which was created."
– Booked Ever After

"A funny read that will have you in stitches."
– Books Are Love

Chapter One

PIPER

The familiar whir of Chicago traffic sounded from below as I sat on my balcony, sipping a cup of coffee, and watching the waves roll in off Lake Michigan. I could barely afford this apartment, but it was worth every penny just to feel this relaxed. It was my one refuge from the world—from my bad memories of Minho dumping me.

Although, I guess "dumping" would've entailed actually talking to me about ending our engagement.

But I found out the hard way. Even now, I couldn't get rid of the image of Hani's legs wrapped around him in *our* car in the alleyway next to the floral shop. There was nothing more final than seeing Minho, or as I liked to refer to him now, Man-Ho, screwing someone else to bring things to an end. Maybe he had some weird Valentine's fetish. First, he was with me, a greeting card writer, who contrived sweet words people couldn't come up with themselves, and then a florist, who pretty much vomited roses, love, and all things Cupid would go crazy for.

With a groan, I shook my head, clearing those visions from my mind. I was not going to spend one more second thinking of that asshat. My lids closed, and when I reopened them, I turned my focus back on the shoreline across the street. Scents of the lake and nearby restaurants wafted in the air, and I inhaled deeply, stretching my legs in front of me. Nope. I'd specifically chosen this location because it was nowhere near our old neighborhood. So, I didn't have to go to the same eateries, or shops, or see the same mutual friends. This was my safe zone.

I set my cup on the glass tabletop. Nothing could ruin this day for me. Nothing. Not even my upcoming meeting at work, to which I still needed to figure out two new Valentine's Day greeting card ideas. These days, it was harder to write about forever love, but if I wanted to keep my job, I had to do it. Besides, even I could BS my way through some sappy thing or another.

In all honesty, it wasn't like I absolutely needed this job because my mom's third husband, and my favorite stepdad of the several I'd had, David, had set up a nice trust fund for me. However, I liked to earn my own way. Not that I didn't appreciate or spend the money he gave me. It was one of the reasons I could afford this place.

"Hey honey, do you want to have breakfast on the balcony today? It's nice out." A familiar voice came from the open door of the apartment next to mine.

No. No freaking way. This was not happening.

Maybe I'd just imagined it since I had been thinking of *him*.

A moment later, I watched in horror as Minho stepped onto the neighboring balcony holding a bowl of rice with eggs on top.

Nope. Didn't imagine it.

Oh God, I couldn't let him see me like this. I smoothed my old nightgown, which had cartoon cats holding coffee cups between their paws on it. Crap. What should I do? Without a second thought, I dropped to my knees, then into a full-blown military crawl, my belly rubbing against the floor, as I used my elbows to propel myself forward across the deck toward my French doors. The only thing worse than a domestic enemy was an asshole ex.

Why? Why? Why? Did God hate me? I mean, seriously. What were the damn odds of my ex moving into the apartment next to mine with his new fiancée?

"Piper? Is that you?" Minho called.

Damn it. I lowered my head and pretended not to hear him while I half-crawled, half-inch-wormed back toward the door. However, as I reached for the handle, still lying on my stomach, the stupid door wouldn't budge. *You've got to be shitting me.* Raising my arm to shield my face, I pushed harder until, at last, it slid open, sending me flying inside.

Maybe he'd think it wasn't me. Maybe he'd believe he just had some weird neighbor lady who liked to slither around on the floor of her deck. And she just happened to look a lot like me.

Sure. He'd definitely believe that.

Who was I kidding? Of course, he'd know it was me. His parents picked these stupid pajamas out for me two Christmases ago. Why didn't I burn them with the rest of the stuff he and the Song family had given me? And why in hell did I wear my damn cat pajamas today of all days? I could've easily opted for the sexy black lace shorts and matching tank. How would he ever regret breaking up with me when I wore childish clothes and didn't brush my hair before I decided to have coffee?

I collapsed on my gray hardwood floor, out of breath from playing leapfrog, and rested my cheek there. Yeah, probably not the most sanitary idea I'd had. Just my luck, I'd breakout in acne or have a dust bunny lodge itself in my throat and kill me.

I squeezed my eyes shut. Death by dust bunny. That sounded nice. Perhaps this was a nightmare. Any moment, I'd wake up and everything would be fine. No ex next door, no shattering of my peaceful world.

The doorbell echoed through my apartment. Frantic, I pulled myself up by the arm of the black leather couch. No. He wouldn't do this to me, would he? Actually ring my doorbell?

Anyone else would've buzzed from the main lobby to be allowed up.

Shaking, I moved toward the door and stared through the peephole.

Sure enough, Minho stood there in his gray suit pants, white dress shirt, and matching gray tie, still looking hot as ever. His dark hair had recently been cut and was styled perfectly as always. His almond-shaped eyes stared intently at the door. He reached for the doorbell again as if his persistence would make me open it. Damn, why couldn't he have gotten ugly in the past year? Like, couldn't God have made him lose all his hair and teeth or given him man boobs or something?

Stepping away from the door, I scurried back to my room. I wasn't ready to face him today. So instead, I hopped in the shower, hoping that when it was time to leave for work, he'd be gone.

After the world's longest shower and enough steam in my bathroom to power a train engine, I finally got dressed, packed my lunch, grabbed my work bag, and headed for the door.

Taking a deep breath, I poked my head out, surveying the area for Minho. When I determined he wasn't in sight, I locked my apartment, then headed down the hall to the elevator at the end.

The bell dinged as the elevator reached my floor, doors opening to an empty car. *Phew,* at least I wouldn't have to talk to anyone. Then I glanced up to see Minho, holding a briefcase and hurrying down the hall.

"Piper. Hey, I thought that was you. Can you hold the door?" he said loudly.

I stared at him a brief moment, my pulse raging in my ears like a too loud rock song at a concert. The doors started to shut. Maybe I could've caught them in time, but I didn't even try.

"Sorry," I called.

Then they closed, and I let out a shaky breath. I wasn't ready for this yet. I didn't want to see him or talk to him or be around him. However, I also wasn't going to be the one to move. This was supposed to be *my* safe haven. My dream home. If he didn't like that we were neighbors, he could move. Or, at least, that's what I told myself.

When I got to the complex lobby, I rushed for the front door, waving to Felix, the doorman, as I passed.

In an attempt to avoid Minho at all costs, I sprinted down the sidewalk. Damn, I better not break an ankle. Heels did not mix with track and field events. But it was desperation that kept me going, even though my lungs and legs were telling me I was in no shape to be running a marathon this morning.

"Hey, Piper," someone called.

I kept moving. There'd be no stopping until I got to All For You Greeting Cards.

"Piper, wait up. Is someone chasing you?"

My gaze shifted to find the marketing director from work, Wooyoung, riding up beside me on his bike. His work bag was strapped around his shoulder and chest.

I swallowed hard, staring at him. His dark hair was styled off his face, his brown eyes nearly hidden behind a pair of black nerdy glasses. His navy blue suit clung to what I assumed was a well-defined body, since all the girls in the office claimed he worked out all the time. Not that I was totally oblivious to how adorable he was, but he just hadn't really registered on my radar. I mean, sure he brought me a coffee every day, but he did that for pretty much everyone. It wasn't like I was special or anything.

"Oh hi," I managed as I slowed down and tried to catch my breath. "No. Um...just trying to get in some exercise before work."

He quirked an eyebrow at me, bringing his bike to a stop. "In heels?"

My cheeks warmed, and I swiped my red hair out of my face and behind my ear. A nervous gesture. "Yeah, you should try it some time. Really builds those leg muscles."

His lips twitched at the corner. "Yeah, I think I'll pass. Heels aren't really my thing."

From behind me, I heard Minho again. Crap. Couldn't he take a hint?

Taking a deep breath, I jumped onto the pegs on the back of Wooyoung's bike. "Go. Go. Go." I tapped his back.

Wooyoung peered at me, but then started peddling.

Falling forward, I clasped his waist, praying I didn't fall off the back, or get a heel caught in the spokes or something. He sped down the side of the street, me hanging on for dear life.

After a couple of blocks, he pulled up in front of a coffee shop and parked his bike while I hopped off.

"What was that about?" His curious gaze met mine.

"My ex. Kind of long story...I'm just not ready to face him."

He nodded. "Okay. Well, I'm pretty sure we lost him. Are you fine with me making a coffee stop?"

"Yeah. No problem. It's not like you're my taxi driver or something."

I followed him into the small café. The scent of coffee and baked goods enveloped me. Damn, I could really use a Long John donut. But the question was, did I "need" it? Probably not.

Wooyoung went to the counter, and the barista smiled at him. Her eyes lit up as she glanced between us. "Oh, my gosh, is this caramel, mocha, latte girl?"

Wooyoung chuckled, his face pinkening. "Yes."

Her smile widened. "I get it now. Good choice." She winked at him.

My gaze shifted between them. What in the heck were they talking about?

The barista set two cups on the counter and took Wooyoung's money from him.

He held out one of the cups for me. "Your favorite, caramel, mocha latte."

"Thanks. How much do I owe you?"

"Nothing." He fell in beside me as we made our way outside to the sidewalk again.

"Seriously, you get me one every day. It's got to get expensive."

He grinned. "Not a big deal. Besides, if it makes you smile, then that's all the payment I need."

I nearly choked on my drink. "Is that a line or something?"

His face turned red, and he ran a hand haphazardly through his hair. "No, I um... Hey, I'll see you at work, okay? Good luck with the rest of your jog."

He hopped on his bike and raced off ahead of me like someone had lit his butt cheeks on fire. What had gotten into him?

When I arrived at the office, Kerrie Holloway, one of our newest sales reps, waved at me from next to the potted baby rose bush in the lobby. Yes, the company owner's Valentine's Day obsession knew no bounds. Kerrie adjusted her black skirt and smoothed her light blue flower-patterned shirt, which bulked from beneath her dark suit jacket. Her brown curly hair was pulled back in a ponytail, making her look younger than forty-three.

"Good, you're here. Mr. Dancy's ready to start our meeting."

"Our meeting?" I squeaked. "Crap. I don't have my cards done. I was gonna work on them this morning, and then Minho showed up. I swear, it's like he can't stop ruining my life."

"Wait. Back up." Kerrie grabbed my arm, tugging me to a stop next to my office. "Minho stopped by?"

"It's worse than that. I'm pretty sure he moved in next door."

"And I thought my morning was bad. Are you alright?"

Sucking in a deep breath, I glanced at her. "I'm not sure."

"Ladies, let's go, our meeting is about to start." Mr. Dancy poked his head out of our conference room, his brown tweed jacket in need of a "this century" makeover.

This day was about to get even better, I was sure.

Shoving my office door open, I tossed my bag inside, grabbed a binder and pen from my desk, and headed into the meeting. I found a seat next to Kerrie and across from Wooyoung, who wouldn't even meet my eye.

Mr. Dancy cleared his throat, scouring the room and staring down the rest of my Valentine's Day and Sweetest Day card team.

Carlos glowered out the window, while Maude, the oldest living creature in the building, took a sip of tea from her mug, leaving behind a too-pink lipstick print. Her white hair reminded me of a cotton ball, while her horn-rimmed glasses perched on her nose like a librarian scowling at patrons.

"Nice that you could all finally join me. Our mandatory meetings are just that, mandatory. So, let's get rolling with your ideas for next year's Valentine's Day cards. Carlos, why don't we start with your art and photos."

Carlos stood, his normally sleek look marred by wrinkled trousers, the same red shirt he'd worn yesterday, and a face that appeared to have not been shaved recently.

"This is all I have." Carlos lined up photos and drawings of flames. "I call it the 'Love is Hell' collection. For all those no-good bastards who dump their loved ones and move to Paris without them."

"Amen to that." I raised my coffee in a toast.

"Yes, nothing says love like hellish flames," Mr. Dancy snapped. "Piper?"

I snorted. "Well, if you loved Carlos's art, then you'll love my idea. How about something more anti-Valentine's, like 'Drunk Butt-Dial cards.' You can make it where the buyer can record their voice, tell their ex what they really think about them, and send it out. Put a little phone on the front, so when it opens, you hear it dial, then ring, maybe even a scratch and sniff beer sticker or something to make it more realistic."

Kerrie busted out laughing, then quickly covered her mouth.

Mr. Dancy turned a shade of red I'd never seen before, something between the hellish flames Carlos had created and the color of an overripe tomato about to explode. "What the hell has gotten into you guys? This isn't a joke. We need to have all our next season's cards ready to go. Maude, please tell me you have something so I can leave this meeting feeling like at least one of our staff knows how to do their job and not put our company under."

Maude smiled. "Of course." She slid a small stack of papers over to him. "Here are a few of my ideas."

Mr. Dancy collected the sheets and read through them. He smiled. "Yes. I love these. Flowers. Love. Forever. This—this is what you guys should be writing about and designing cards for." He tossed them down in front of me. "Maybe read up on it. I'm calling this meeting to an end and warning you now. You better come prepared next time."

I stood, ready to filter from the room with everyone else, but Mr. Dancy blocked my way.

"Not so fast, Piper. Sit." He pointed at the chair I'd just vacated.

"Sir, look, I can explain everything..."

"Piper, listen. You are a very talented writer, it's one of the reasons I originally hired you. I know you've had a really rough year, but you have to get back on top of things here, otherwise, I'm afraid, I might have to find someone else. Someone who doesn't think the answer to Valentine's Day is a beer-scented sticker."

I nodded. "I promise, I'll have something to you soon."

After he left, I stared out the window at the sky. *You have to get it together, girl. You can't lose this job because Manho decided to break up with you. You can't let him win and see how unhappy you are.*

If I didn't have motivation before to get over him, I sure did now. Cynical as I was, I'd find a way to create a love-themed card, even if I had to spend the next seventy-two hours watching rom-com movies and eating a tub of chocolate ice cream.

Chapter Two

KERRIE

"Mom, Tommy stole the peanut butter from me," Nella hollered from down the hall.

I groaned. "You guys, I don't have time for your fighting this morning. We're already running behind schedule. Sophie, can you help them make their lunches?" I poked my head out of the bathroom, searching for my oldest child. "Soph?"

"She left already," Nella said. "Mya picked her up. I forgot to tell you."

Of course, Sophie left. Ever since she turned sixteen last year, it was like she had to test every rule in the house. And since Hal, my ex-husband, or pseudo ex-husband, or whatever he was now—roommate, live-in pain-in-the-ass—wasn't here in the mornings now, she kind of did what she wanted. Not that the kids knew we were divorced. Hal didn't want to be painted in a bad light as the one who ruined our family. The very man I'd been married to for twenty years, who'd told me he was bored with me and wanted something different, or rather, something younger with perkier boobs or whatever it was he was looking for in the women he snuck into the house.

Nope. He didn't want to be the bad guy, so even his family didn't know about our split. Just me. His ex "not ex."

Of course, I didn't like this arrangement, but when you spend your entire marriage as a stay-at-home mom, never working outside the house, it's hard to find a job, even with a college degree. Although, being a stay-at-home mom was probably the hardest job on the planet, just not one that included a paycheck. So, I was in this "fake marriage" for financial purposes. At least, until I was able to put some money away to get a different place for me and the kids.

Tommy bounded down the hall, jarring me from my thoughts, peanut butter glopped on his hand with Nella in pursuit. I reached out to grab hold of his arm, but instead, he wrapped himself around my leg, leaving a messy brown handprint on my work pants.

Ugh. I didn't have time for this. I couldn't be late for work, not while I was still in the probationary period. My ninetieth day was next Thursday.

"Shit! Enough," I shouted. "We don't play in the peanut butter, Tommy. Get in the bathroom and wash your hands. Now."

He peered up at me. "Shit. Shit. Shit."

"Don't say that word."

"You did."

"That's because I'm the mom. Just please be good."

"You used to be nicer in the morning. Now you're mean," he said, tears welling in his eyes.

I sighed. "Well, I used to not have to work, buddy. Now I do. I'm sorry I yelled, but you know better. Get cleaned up while I go change into something else. And don't touch the peanut butter again. I'll make your lunch when I'm done."

Running down the hall, I barged into my room. What did I even have clean? I scoured my closet until I found a black skirt hanging up. I wasn't even sure if it'd still fit me. I couldn't remember the last time I wore it. Had I ever worn it? I glanced at the designer tag and frowned. Was it even mine or one of Hal's new girlfriends'? Right now, I couldn't exactly be picky. I had to have something clean to put on that didn't smell like I'd rolled around on the lunchroom floor.

Groaning, I whipped off my pants, tossed them in the hamper in the corner of the room, which at the moment was overflowing with clothes, then unzipped the skirt and tugged it. Only it didn't go all the way up.

"Come on, please. Can one thing just go right?" I jerked on the waistband again, jumping up and down until it skimmed up over my hips. Okay. I could make this work. As long as I didn't breathe or have to bend over, I'd be fine. Except for the fact the zipper wouldn't close.

Damn it.

Wait, maybe I had some Spanx or something. I shimmied over to my dresser drawer, pushing my underwear and bras aside. Nope. No Spanx. They were probably in the dirty laundry, too.

With a sigh, I fell backward onto the bed, hoping laying down would do the trick. I sucked in my gut. The zipper moved. Yes! This was good. Just a little more. I sucked in more. Finally, it was all the way up. Once it was secured, I attempted to sit up, trying to ignore the roll of fat which now overhung the waistband. It was so noticeable in this shirt. And I felt like, at any moment now, I might actually be cut in half by the tight fabric.

"Beauty is pain," I whispered. Or rather, a two sizes too small skirt was. Reaching for a suit jacket to try and hide my mid-section, I threw it on, then raced back to the kitchen to finish getting the kids ready.

After I had everyone's lunches made, school clothes on, and backpacks prepared, I ushered the kids into the minivan, which at the moment had Fruit Loops crunched into the backseat carpet as well as a chocolate milk stain on the seat from Tommy. Things I used to be able to clean up right away, but now didn't have time to do. If the carpool moms saw my vehicle now, they'd probably call CPS on me or something.

"Mooooooooom, I was supposed to bring something for show and tell today," Nella said. "I won't get another chance again until next month." Her voice quivered, a clear sign she was about to burst out crying.

"Here, take this." I handed my purse back to her, trying not to drive into oncoming traffic. "See if you can find mini-Nella." A doll I'd bought for her birthday, which had a freaky resemblance to her, but sounded demonic when you pushed a button on its back.

"I'm not finding her..."

"Well, see if there's something else in there."

A buzzing, vibrating sound came from the backseat. "Whoa, what's this?" Nella held up something pink in my peripheral vision.

Oh, hell. How did she find that? I purposely kept it with me so the kids wouldn't see it. "I...it's a flashlight."

"I don't see a light."

"That's not a flashlight, it's a lightsaber," Tommy said. "Let me see it." He proceeded to make the sounds of a lightsaber slicing the air with my pink vibrator.

"Give it back! I get to take the flashlight with me. Mom said I could find a show and tell thing in her purse."

Thwack!

"Ow, Mom, Nella hit me with the lightsaber." Tommy's voice quivered. "That hurt my face."

Dear Lord, please save me. "Nella, just give that here." I turned in my seat and ripped it from her hand.

"Hey, I was going to bring that!"

"Not a good idea. Why don't you keep looking," I said, face on fire.

I heard her unzip the front pocket. "Oh, hey, mini-Nella's right here." She laughed, tossing my purse back into the front seat. "Thanks, Mama."

Hal never had to deal with any of this. Not peanut butter hands, or mouthy sixteen-year-olds, or kids finding vibrators in secret purse pockets. He got to just "play" Dad. He pretty much came and went as he wanted. All he had to do was tell the kids he was working out of town, then take off and leave everything to me.

When we pulled up to a stop light, I leaned over and threw the adult toy into my glove box. Hopefully it'll be safe there. I needed a drink, and it was only seven-forty-five. After long minutes in traffic, I finally dropped the kids off at school, then headed into work.

By some miracle, I made it in time, even beating most of my coworkers there. I hung out, waiting for Piper, my new best friend. Although, she was quite a bit younger than me being only twenty-six, we shared one common bond. We were both the product of recent breakups.

She was someone I could talk to on my lunch hour and bitch about Hal. Even though she didn't know the part where he had other women in our house. It wasn't something I could just bring up to people. It was bad enough hiding our divorce, but to have everyone think me weak for not just moving out was hard.

Piper didn't judge me about still sharing our residence. Of course, she didn't know all the grizzly details. Maybe someday, I'd tell her.

Just then, Piper rushed in, carrying her messenger bag, red hair flying behind her like a cape, seeming more flustered than normal. Perhaps I wasn't the only one having a bad morning.

But before we could actually talk, Mr. Dancy appeared like a wizard in a fantasy movie, ushering us all into the meeting room for what I was sure would be a long one. I wasn't even certain why I had to go today. He didn't have any sales numbers or anything having to do with my department on the list, other than I was assigned to the Valentine's Day team.

It took all of two seconds for Mr. Dancy to flip out after getting everyone gathered. First, Carlos with his 'Love is Hell' line of cards, then Piper with her greeting cards for exes.

My hands twisted nervously in my lap, hoping he didn't call on me for something, too. Like instead of sales, he'd assign me my own line of cards. Maybe the 'I don't know how to breakup' ones?

"Oh. My. God. I have to get my shit together," Piper said, sliding into my office after the meeting. "I'm one more bad idea away from Mr. Dancy firing me." She plopped into the chair across from me and leaned her head on top of my desk.

"Everything will be fine. You'll see," I said.

"I don't know anymore. I mean, look at my luck. Who the hell has their ex move in next door to them with their new fiancé?" She sighed.

"Hey, at least you don't still live with your ex. Hal has all the benefits of having me as a live-in wife, other than the whole sex thing."

"Yeah, but you said it's amicable and not too bad. This is being forced on me."

I chewed my bottom lip. They all thought I had it great. That Hal and I were actually still friends. They didn't know how much the divorce hurt or how hard it was lying to my kids. Would it be bad for one person to know the truth?

Yes, it would. At least, right now. Perhaps I'd feel better about telling someone once I was able to save up some more money, so I could at least say I planned on moving out and stopping the charade.

"Okay, let's not talk about exes until lunch. Why ruin our mornings further? Besides, at least you didn't have your kid try to bring your vibrator for show and tell, and the other pretend he was in the middle of a lightsaber battle."

Piper grinned, then burst out laughing. "You're kidding?"

"No. I wish I was."

"What did you do?"

"Told them it was a flashlight." My nose wrinkled. "And it is now hidden away in my car's glove box."

"That is classic." She picked a pen up off my desk and clicked the top of it, then proceeded to draw hearts on a sticky note.

"I swear this stuff only happens to me." My fingers wrapped around my coffee mug, and I picked it up, taking a swig of lukewarm coffee.

"Hey, on the bright side, you didn't have your ex see you in cartoon cat pajamas crawling across your deck." She winced. "Sorry, forgot we weren't talking about exes. It's just, I'm still freaking over this."

"Maybe he was just there visiting or something," I offered.

"No, I don't think so. Ugh, I swear."

Mr. Dancy walked past my door.

"We should probably get to work," I whispered.

Piper's eyes widened, and she hopped to her feet. "Yeah, I'm in enough trouble. I'll see you at lunch."

She scurried from the room and raced across the hall to her office.

With a sigh, I pulled up last year's sales reports to start figuring out what Valentine's Cards worked for the company, and which ones fizzled. Four hours and three cups of coffee later, I had the numbers on a spreadsheet.

My stomach growled, but food would have to wait until after I used the ladies' room. Heading down the hallway, I went into the bathroom. I unzipped my skirt, letting my bottom extremities get blood to them. Damn, it was good to feel my midsection again. When I finished, I flushed the toilet, then proceeded to tug the fabric up around my thighs and hips.

My fingers closed around the metal clasp of the zipper, and I tugged. Only it wouldn't go up. Crap. I knew I shouldn't have undone it, but I'd had to go so bad, and the waistband had dug so far into my midsection, I couldn't breathe any longer.

I eyed the floor. No way in hell could I lay down on the tile. Who knew what gross things might be on it or how often the janitors cleaned it.

Desperate, I moved to the door and peered down the hallway, spotting Piper heading for the cafeteria.

"Piper," I hollered.

She turned to face me. "Hey, are you going to lunch?"

"I...yeah, but I have a slight problem. Can you come here a second?" My face burned, but it was either ask her for help, or not zip my skirt.

"Hey, what's up?" She came inside the bathroom with me.

"I can't get this up." I pointed at the back of me, where my white granny panties were showing. Not my most defining moment.

"Here, move away from the door. I'll try to pull it up while you hold the fabric together."

She tugged at it, jumping up and down in the process, much like I had this morning when trying to do this myself.

"Wait, I think it moved," I said.

"Alright, I'm going to squish you against the sink a second with my hips to see if that helps. I need more leverage."

"I think I'm almost there."

"Can you do it a little more?"

"What in God's name are you two doing?" Maude's raspy voice called from behind us. "Dear Jesus in Heaven. Are you two lesbians now? I never saw it coming the way you carried on about your exes."

Heat flared over my body. "No, this isn't what it looks like. I-I'm having issues with my skirt."

"Trust me, I'm all about the men," Piper said. "I mean, I'm not like *all* about them in a slutty way...I—"

Maude snorted. "I don't really care about your love lives. I just need to use the bathroom. So, whatever it is that's going on between you, if you could take it outside."

The stall door slammed shut, and Maude hummed while she used the bathroom.

In the meantime, Piper gave my zipper one last yank, and it finally went back into place.

"There, it's all set now," Piper said.

"Good. I think I worked up an appetite."

"Me, too. Let's wash our hands and get some food. So, next time, we're going to do this in your car, right?" She winked.

From inside the stall, Maude gasped.

My lips twitched. "Yeah, definitely in my car. I've actually never done it in a vehicle before."

If Maude wanted to eavesdrop on everything we said, then let her try and figure out what she'd really walked in on. I swear, that old broad was always so nosey. Now, we better pray she didn't try to talk to Mr. Dancy about what she 'might' have seen, or Piper and I might be looking for new jobs.

Chapter Three

MAUDE

My light blue heels clicked on the hardwood floor as I made my way out into the kitchen. Tiny glass roosters decorated the tops of the cupboards, staring back at me with the same glass smiles they'd had for decades. We still had the red and white checkerboard tile backsplash we'd installed when we'd moved into the house. Same suburban home, white picket fence, and small backyard. Nothing had changed in all that time.

Corny stood at the stove frying up the last of the bacon, hash browns, and eggs—our morning ritual breakfast. Surprisingly, neither of us have had a heart attack yet.

"Smells good, sweets," I said, pouring us both a cup of coffee and carrying it to the table.

He turned to glance at me. His gray hair was unruly as always, the playful grin pasted on a now wrinkled face. "Looking beautiful, my Maude-Belle." The same line he'd told me every morning for the last fifty years.

You'd think I'd get sick of hearing it, but I didn't. Cornelius "Corny" was the love of my life. Sure, we got annoyed with one another sometimes. Like when he left his dentures on the counter in the bathroom or forgot to change out the roll of toilet paper or took an hour on the shitter reading the paper. But those were just small issues.

He pressed a kiss to my temple, setting my plate of food in front of me. "Better eat up. We're running late."

My eyes narrowed as I tried to make out the numbers on the clock. Damn eyes. With a grunt, I grabbed my glasses and slid them on my face. "Ah, how did we get so far behind schedule?"

He snorted. "You changed your clothes three times, Maude. Then you said your hair was too poofy because of the curlers you left in last night."

"Never you mind. Just shovel that food in so we can go." I took a forkful of eggs and gobbled them up.

"What do you want me to bring you for lunch today?" Corny asked, sopping up some of the runny egg yolk with his toast.

My hand patted his arm. "Whatever you'd like."

He'd retired about ten years ago from the post office. Ever since then, he came to the greeting card company to have lunch with me. Most of the girls in the office were jealous. They didn't have husbands or boyfriends who cooked for them, let alone visited them at work on a regular basis.

Nope. What we had was special. Unbreakable. Unlike all these young people throwing away their marriages at the first sign of trouble. Corny and I had been through everything together: A war overseas, the loss of our son when he was only twenty, going to jail for participating in the Civil Rights Movement, the deaths of our siblings… We'd survived it all.

I planned to be with this man until we both died. Well, if I didn't kill him first. "Quit smacking your lips together." I swatted his arm. "You know I hate it when you do that."

He chuckled, shoving more toast in his mouth. "That's why I do it. Can't have you getting too comfortable." Corny stopped chewing and winced, rubbing his eyes.

"Are you alright?"

He nodded, replacing his frown with a thin smile. "I'm fine, sweets. I've had a headache since I woke up. It's damn near making my vision blurry."

"Where are your glasses?"

"On the counter. I'll grab 'em before we leave." He waved me off as if I was a pesky mosquito.

Once we finished our food, I washed the few dishes in the sink while Corny fed the cat and put our bills out in the mailbox.

Ten minutes later, we were in the car heading into Chicago and all the blasted traffic. This was the only part of the morning I hated—the rude drivers honking and cutting us off. The people who couldn't take their heads out of their phones for two seconds to make sure they weren't walking off the sidewalk into traffic.

"So many idiots wandering about today," I said, shaking my head at a man who'd just stuck his middle finger up at us. "Same to you."

Corny smiled. "You know, we should have you start driving once or twice a week."

I frowned. "No. I'm fine with you doing it."

His hand clutched mine and he gave it a squeeze. "You haven't really been behind the wheel much. Not since I retired. I think it'd be good to keep in practice."

"No amount of asking is going to change my mind."

Why was he bringing this up all of a sudden? Not that I should be surprised. We often had talks about what we'd do if the other one wasn't around. I mean, we were at an age now where we had to. We weren't trying to be morbid, but there were certain things you realized as you got older. Things didn't always work like they used to. Sometimes, you needed pills for stuff you never thought you would. You didn't wear sexy clothes any longer. Hell, I was lucky if I could keep my boobs from hitting my knees. That's why I got me one of those support bras. Nothing sexy about it—just doing its job.

Corny didn't have teeth that were his own anymore, and I better not sneeze or laugh too hard, or I might pee my pants. Yeah, growing old wasn't all it was cracked up to be, but it was better than the alternative.

"Have it your way, Maude-Belle." He sighed, pulling into the All For You Greeting Card Company parking lot.

"I usually do," I said, planting a kiss on his cheek before climbing from the car. "I'll see you at lunch."

He nodded. "Yep, see you then. Oh, before I forget to tell you, I have a med-check appointment with Doctor Fleming later this afternoon, but I'll be out in plenty of time to pick you up tonight."

With one last wave, I filtered into the red bricked building, and went straight for my office. The company had been in this same place since it opened, although, now there were many more businesses and apartments surrounding it. I'd been one of the first employees Mr. Dancy hired. Most card companies hired people to work from their homes to create their cards, paying them a certain amount per word, but not Mr. Dancy. He wanted a more personalized touch. He was of the opinion that by having staff all gathered in one place, brainstorming and interacting would give his cards more feeling. So far, he'd stayed open, even after the surge of online greeting cards.

My office was hotter than the bowels of hell this morning, meaning Mr. Dancy probably had the air conditioning turned down to conserve money. The man was more frugal than me, which said a lot.

"Don't forget, we have a meeting." Mr. Dancy stuck his head in my office. "Seems like everyone else is running late."

I snorted. "The young never respect timeliness."

"We're a dying breed, Maude." He sighed, adjusting his tweed suit jacket, which I was certain he'd had since the start of the company. He called it his lucky suit. I called it his 'only suit.'

Grabbing my large coffee mug, I went to the break room to fill it. Wooyoung stood at the sink, his eyes closed.

"Are you meditating over the dishes?"

He spun around. His dark hair brushed back from his face, revealing sculpted cheek bones. He laughed. "No. Contemplating my life choices."

"Oh?" I said, reaching for the coffee pot.

"I actually talked to Piper this morning. Only I flaked, then rode off, leaving her stranded at the café."

My lips twitched. Of course, Wooyoung had been smitten with Piper since day one of her employment here, but she was clueless to his constant attempts to get her attention. Too caught up in her ex. She and Kerrie both. All they did every lunch hour was gripe about their exes.

If Piper opened her eyes, she'd have a great catch in Wooyoung. He reminded me of Corny. The way he always brought her coffee, or left chocolates on her desk. How he held the door open for her and complimented her. The girl was blind.

"Ah, what you need is a love coach, boy," I said.

He quirked a perfect eyebrow at me. If I was fifty years younger and not married, I'd fall head over heels for him myself.

"A love coach?" He chuckled. "That sounds kind of desperate."

I laughed. "Well, desperate times call for desperate measures. Besides, I wouldn't recommend just anyone. You know, I've got lots of experience in the love department. Been married fifty years. So, I figure I could help you out. I know both you and Piper. She needs a good guy in her life."

He rubbed the back of his neck. "Like what kind of help are you suggesting?"

"For starters, we have to get you talking to her more, and I can give you nudges when you lose courage, that sort of thing," I said. "They don't call me Dr. Greeting Card for no reason, you know."

"Okay, but she can't know you're helping me," he said, peering around as if to make sure no one listened to our conversation.

"I promise."

"Okay, then we have a deal." He shook my hand, then hurried from the lounge.

With my caffeine refilled, I headed to my office where I gathered my ideas for our meeting, which turned out to be a huge disaster. Not only was I the only one prepared, but everyone else had seemingly lost their minds. The Valentine's line had turned into a 'jaded lover' track in under thirty seconds.

Mr. Dancy rarely got mad, but today, the man looked like he might maim someone. Not wanting to be included in his wrath, I rushed from the conference room as soon as he said the meeting was over.

I got my computer up and running, and clicked open the folder of ideas I had, but before I could start writing, Mr. Dancy came in, shut the door, and sat down.

"Maude, I swear we're the only two sane people left in this building. Am I being unreasonable? Too demanding?"

My fingers picked at a string on my light blue skirt. "No, sir. You just have to realize we're dealing with a different generation. They're far more cynical and spoiled. They don't know what hard work really is."

He nodded. "The thing is, I know Piper is an excellent writer. Her cards, prior to her fiancé leaving, were selling like air conditioners in a heat wave."

I snorted. Too bad he didn't run the one at the company during a heat wave. "I agree, she's talented." And was also my biggest competition here.

"She is. Which is why I need your help, Maude. Maybe there's something you could say or do to get her back on track."

The coffee I'd just sucked down, got stuck in my throat, causing me to sputter. "Um...I'm not sure I'm the right person for that."

"Of course, you are. You've been married forever. Perhaps she could join you and Cornelius during some lunches, get a feel for what real love is. It might spark something within her." He clapped his hands together like he'd solved the world's toughest riddle.

Hot damn. It was bad enough listening to her and Kerrie complain during their lunches, but to have her join me and ruin my day, too? But then again, it might help on the Wooyoung front. I could have them both eat with us, give them some time to bond.

"I'll try my best," I said.

"Thank you, Maude. I owe you big." He rose and left the room.

What in the world did I just agree to? Sucking in a deep breath, I pulled up a new blank document on my computer and typed at the top. "How to Get Piper Writing About Love."

I was gonna have my work cut out for me.

After working diligently on my list of ideas for a few hours, I glanced up to see it was time for lunch. Corny would probably be here any minute. So, I went to the bathroom, and walked in on something I wasn't sure I should see.

Kerrie was pressed against the sink with Piper behind her, her hands shoved in her skirt.

No wonder Wooyoung couldn't make progress with Piper. She was a lesbian. How had I missed this before?

"Dear Jesus in Heaven. Are you two lesbians now? I never saw it coming the way you carried on about your exes," I said.

"No, this isn't what it looks like. I...I'm having issues with my skirt," Kerrie said, her face reddening.

"Trust me, I'm all about the men," Piper said. "I mean, I'm not like *all* about them in a slutty way...I—"

"I don't really care about your love lives. I just need to use the bathroom. So, whatever it is that's going on between you, if you could take it outside." I tried to get into the stall as quickly as I could.

The door slammed shut, and I hummed as loud as I could, wanting to drown out anything else that might be going on.

"There, it's all set now," Piper said.

"Good. I think I worked up an appetite," Kerrie answered.

"Me, too. Let's wash our hands and get some food. So, next time, we're going to do this in your car, right?"

A gasp escaped my lips before I could stop it. Wooyoung and I were going to have to have a conversation during lunch.

Once they left, I hurried to wash my hands, then went to find Corny, who waited in the lobby for me. He had a bag filled with Tupperware containers.

"Maude-Belle, brought your favorite chicken sandwich today." He kissed my cheek, taking my free hand in his and walking with me to the cafeteria.

We found a table near the back, but unfortunately, Piper and Kerrie took the one near ours.

"We're going to have someone joining us for lunch today," I said. Although, at the moment, I didn't want to be the one breaking Wooyoung's heart. But it had to be done.

"Who's that?"

"Wooyoung, he's the Korean-American boy I told you about."

He chuckled. "Are you getting a crush on him?"

"No. I was supposed to help him land her." I gestured to Piper. "But I'm not so sure that's going work now."

A second later, Wooyoung sauntered in and came to sit with me and my husband. I slid my glasses off my face and rubbed my eyes, then turned to him.

"Wooyoung, I'm afraid I might have some bad news on the Piper front," I said, not wasting any time.

He frowned. "What's going on?" He took a bite of salad.

"How do I say this," I muttered. "I'm just going to be straight with you, kid. Piper and Kerrie are lesbians."

Wooyoung spat his food out of his mouth and started laughing. "Those two?"

"I, well…I walked in on them in the bathroom."

"Are you sure you didn't misunderstand something?"

My lids shut. "Trust me, kid, there are some things you can't unsee." Boy, did I wish I could. I didn't want to be the bearer of bad news. However, if Piper once liked guys, maybe she would again. We might have our work cut out for us.

Chapter Four

PIPER

I unwrapped my turkey sandwich and glanced over to where Maude sat with her husband. The truth was, I used to think it was cute how Cornelius came to have lunch with her every day, but more and more lately, it seemed like they were rubbing their perfect relationship in our faces.

My gaze flitted to Wooyoung, who sat down with them, which was a new development. He normally ate with a couple of guys from the art department. Maybe Maude planned on adopting him or something.

"So, what are you going to do about Minho? You can't exactly avoid your apartment forever," Kerrie said, taking a bite of salad.

"Are you sure? Because I could totally just spend the night in my office."

"And roast your ta-tas off? You know Mr. Dancy doesn't believe in air conditioning. One night in here, and you'll die of heat stroke."

"Good point. Damn. Why did my ex have to move in next door? Is there nothing sacred in this world any longer?"

"Nope. Love is a joke. A myth. It's not real." Kerrie waved a stick of celery around like a wand. "There are no Prince Charmings in the world."

"You two shouldn't be so cynical. You're far too young for that," Maude said from the table beside ours. "So, quit your whining and get back on the horse. There are plenty of MEN out there to date."

My face flushed. Oh God, she'd actually believed the thing in the bathroom with Kerrie happened.

"Well, not all of us have had the luxury of being married since the flood," I snapped.

Her husband chuckled. "Ignore my wife. She likes to stick her nose in where it doesn't belong. There's nothing wrong with being single."

"Is that so?" Maude glowered at him. "Perhaps I should show you how great single life is, you traitor. You should side with your wife." She turned to stare at Wooyoung.

Wooyoung held his hands up. "I'm Switzerland. I'm staying out of this."

"You can't always avoid conflict," I said. "You should choose a side."

He rubbed the back of his neck, his gaze softening. "I think, in a way, Maude is right. Why waste time dwelling on jerks? There are so many other things you could be doing."

My fingers gripped my fork tighter. "Like?"

"I...um."

Maude nudged his shoulder. What was she even doing?

"Like grabbing a bite to eat with me after work? Then you won't have to go home right away." He glanced down at the table, then to Maude, and back to me again.

Whoa. I hadn't expected that. Had Maude put him up to it? Maybe she felt sorry for me and decided to play matchmaker. However, if it meant not going home right away, I was in.

"Sure," I agreed.

"Great, I'll meet you in front of the building after work." He hopped up, not even finishing his food, and hurried out of the cafeteria.

Kerrie's eyes widened as she stared at me. "So, that was unexpected. Did you know he had a thing for you?"

"I didn't. Although, do you think Maude put him up to it? Maybe she just wanted to test us to see if we were really lesbians. What if he doesn't show?"

"Now you're being paranoid." Kerrie swigged her diet cola.

"Am I?"

Mr. Dancy came tromping through. "You ladies need to turn your office lights off when you're not in them. Do you know how much electricity costs in this building? Money doesn't grow on trees."

He walked past us toward the cafeteria line. I watched as he pulled packets of salt and pepper from his pockets to add to the contents set out in baskets on the counter. Packets he'd most certainly swiped from restaurants, I was sure. The man was like Scrooge to the nth power. It was hard to believe he owned his own business.

Shaking my head, I turned back to Kerrie. "So, you think me going on a date with Wooyoung is a good idea?"

"Yes. The man is hot. I mean, have you ever seen the muscle definition when he takes his suit jacket off? Half of the people in the building are in love with him. But he's oblivious. Kind of like someone else I know." She smiled, nudging me with her elbow.

"Who?"

"You. That man has been bringing you coffee every day. He's also the one who anonymously leaves you candy on your desk. It's seriously adorable."

"No. He does that for everyone."

"Actually, he doesn't. You're the only one. I promise."

"Oh." My teeth grazed my bottom lip. How did I not see that? My pulse quickened. Maybe that's what the barista meant earlier.

"Yeah, *oh*." She laughed, peering at her watch. "Crap, we should probably get back to work. Don't need boss man firing us."

"Well, in case I don't talk to you before I leave, wish me luck tonight."

"Everything will be fine. Don't worry."

I sighed. "I hope so. I mean, I'm not exactly experienced on the guy front. Minho and I were together from Junior high until last year."

"All the more reason to go with Wooyoung. Enjoy yourself. You deserve this."

Of course, Kerrie was right. It'd be good for me to move on. But dating a coworker could turn out to be problematic. What if things went to hell? Or I totally botched our date? I'd have to see him every day. At least with Minho, I could semi avoid him.

"Quit psyching yourself out," Kerrie said, following me from the cafeteria.

"What? I didn't even say anything."

She laughed again. "You didn't have to. One look at your face, and I can see the wheels turning."

I rolled my eyes, tucking my lunch box under my arm. "Maybe we really should date. You can read me better than anyone else."

Kerrie raised an eyebrow. "Don't say that too loud or Maude might jump to more conclusions."

Back in my office, I sat in front of my computer. Had I really agreed to dinner with Wooyoung? My hand rested against my chest, the thudding of my heart making my fingers jump. Giving my head a shake, I focused on the screen.

My cards weren't going to write themselves. Let's see...

Your love is like a sunrise, always rising above the sea,

Your love is like a beacon, always here to guide me...

Holy crap. The words were flowing. They were back. Wait, was this because of Wooyoung? But as I sat trying to finish it, my thoughts stumbled.

Whyyyy.

"Come on, girl, you can do this. What comes next?"

Broken hearts. Loss. Alone. Cheating ass fiancés.

For a few hours, I sat there, trying to bring back whatever spark of inspiration I'd had. However, I realized those fleeting thoughts were long gone. After putting my flash-drive in, I hit Save. At least I had a start to something. More than I'd been able to come up with in a while.

After shutting everything down, I packed my bag and headed out of my office. There, standing in the lobby, was Wooyoung. His broad shoulders nearly blocked out the light of the window, his dark hair a little more unruly than it had been this morning. He took his glasses off and rubbed his eyes. As if sensing my ogling, he glanced at me. A smile lit his face, nearly igniting me.

Geez. How had I not realized how hot he was before?

"Hey." He waved.

"Hey." A blush crept up the back of my neck like a spider on the prowl.

"So, when I asked you to dinner tonight, I forgot, I brought my bike to work." Wooyoung shrugged.

I laughed. "Well, as you know, I don't mind hitching a ride on it."

"True. If you want, we can take it back to my apartment and I can trade it out for my car. Or we can ride over to the pub from here for burgers. I mean, if you eat meat."

"There are very few foods I don't like." I patted my belly. "And I'm fine taking your bike over. It's kind of fun."

He chuckled. "Maybe I should invest in a tandem bike."

"But then that would mean *I'd* have to exercise."

"What happened to the high-heeled track star from this morning?" He quirked an eyebrow at me.

I followed him out the door to the bicycle rack where he had his bike locked up. "She's still trying to find her lungs, which I'm pretty sure are outside my apartment building in a pile of ash. Not to mention, I think I might have a blister."

"I'll have to get you some good tennis shoes." He grinned, hopping onto his bike. Once he was settled, I climbed on behind him.

My arms laced around his mid-section. For a second, I attempted to keep some space between us, but I quickly learned there was no way to ride a bike together without physically pressing close. Breast to back, my head to his shoulder. My breathing hitched, but as I inhaled deeply, I was rewarded with the scent of his cologne. He turned slightly, his cheek brushing against mine. My breath caught in my throat at feeling the slight start of stubble.

"You ready?" His voice came out hoarse.

"I—yeah."

He eased us into the bike lane and peddled hard. I loved feeling the way his muscles contracted against me. I closed my eyes and clung tighter. The breeze tugged at my hair while the scents of the city wafted around us. Food. Vehicles. The lake. A giant mixing pot of our city's fragrances.

Soon, we pulled up to O'Vandy's Pub. Wooyoung put his feet down to steady the bike while I hopped off. He then secured it to a nearby pole with a padlock. We both carried our work bags inside with us.

The moment we walked in, the smell of burgers and beer made my mouth water. I didn't drink, except for the rare occasion, but I couldn't resist a good slab of beef. It'd been a while since I'd been here.

A waitress came over. "Welcome to O'Vandy's, where the grill is always sizzling and the brew is always cold. How many in your party tonight?" The girl peered between us, giving her dark hair a toss over her shoulder.

"Two," Wooyoung said.

"Right this way."

She led us through a crowd of people standing and sitting near the big screen watching the baseball game. She sat us toward the back, next to a giant map of Ireland. Dim stained-glass lights hung over the booth, the dark red leather seats cold against my legs.

Once we slid in, she handed us both a menu. "I'll give you a few minutes to look these over and come back to get your order. Do you want me to start you with drinks?"

"I'll have a water with lemon," I said.

"I'll have the same." Wooyoung set his bag beside him, picking up his menu to browse through it.

"Okay. I'll be right back with that."

"Aren't you going to check out the menu?" Wooyoung asked.

I laughed. "I'm a creature of habit. I love their barbeque bacon burger. I get it every time I come here."

"What? You never try anything new? Ah, we must fix that," he said. "You should order one small thing you've never tried before to go with your burger."

"I like to stick with what's safe," I teased. "You see, I already know I like this burger. So, if I order something else, and end up hating it, then I'll still be hungry."

"How about an appetizer? Let's be adventurous." He reached over and pointed to something on my menu. "Let's try this."

"Calamari? Isn't that squid?" My nose wrinkled.

"Yes, but it's deep fried, and see, they make it look like onion rings."

I chewed my bottom lip. "Dang, I can't believe I'm going to let you talk me into this. Fine. I'll try one. But just for the sake of being adventurous. Hopefully, this date doesn't end in a bucket of vomit."

He threw his head back, laughing. "It won't, I promise."

After we ordered, Wooyoung took a sip of his water and stared at me. "So, tell me about your ex?"

My eyes widened. "Wait, what?"

His fingers toyed with the wrapper from his straw. "I figure we can get all the awkward ex talk out of the way now on our first date. That way, every other date we can be focused on us and having fun."

My lips twitched. "You know, normal people don't suggest stuff like that."

"Well, I dare say neither of us is exactly normal..."

"Hey." I tossed my napkin at him. "I'm normal."

"Says the girl who was sprinting in heels this morning and jumped on the back of my bike like you were being chased by the mob."

"Good point. Okay, fine. I just don't want to ruin this."

He reached across the table and took my hand. His skin was warm and soft. "It won't. I've waited a long time to ask you out, and I don't want there to be any barriers in getting to know you better."

"Well, here goes then. Minho and I met in elementary school after his family moved to the U.S. from South Korea. We became fast friends. Basically, I was one of the only ones who didn't pick on him about his English skills," I said. "We started dating in junior high and all through college. Then, our junior year at Roosevelt University, he proposed to me. We decided to wait to set the date until we both got good jobs and were settled in."

"So, he's pretty much been your only boyfriend?" Wooyoung asked, seemingly surprised.

"Yeah. Pathetic, right?"

His thumb brushed against my palm, sending tiny shots of heat through my entire body. But I pulled my hand back, resting it in my lap.

"No. It shows how much you cherish a relationship."

"But it didn't last," I argued. "Last year, I caught him cheating on me. Like, legit caught him. He was in our car, parked in an alley, screwing some florist."

"A florist?"

"Yep. Which is why I kind of have a hate relationship with Valentine's Day now." I moved my cup out of the way as the waitress brought our plates and set them in front of us. "So yeah, those are the gory details of my doomed engagement. How about you."

"Sadly, I've only had two girlfriends. One in high school, who broke up with me when we left for college, and one girlfriend in college, who turned out to be way more into partying than I was. Needless to say, we cut ties after about five months, and me having to bail her out of jail. At that point, I decided I needed to focus on school instead."

"Here's to shitty past relationships," I said, raising my glass.

He clinked his cup against mine. "I'll drink to that. But so you know, going forward, it's not going to be like that."

"Oh?"

"No more bad dates."

"So, you're saying you want to hang out with me again?" I picked up a piece of Calamari, eyeing it. Damn, this thing better not suction to my throat and choke me or something. All I pictured were tentacles trying to kill me like the things you see in sci-fi alien movies.

"Yes. I mean, only if you want to."

I nodded. "I'd like that."

"Are you going to eat that or stare at it?"

"Ah, I don't know. Okay, on the count of three." I closed my eyes. "One. Two. Three." I took a bite of the breaded sea creature. And surprisingly, I didn't die.

"What do you think?"

"Not bad. I was picturing something a lot more deadly." My lids opened to find him watching me with his mocha-colored eyes.

"See, trying new things isn't always bad."

Somehow, I got the feeling he wasn't talking just about the food. Maybe he was right.

When we finished eating, Wooyoung led me back to his bike. After we were both secured in place, he peddled us to my building.

"Did you want to come up for a second? If nothing else, I've got a great view of Lake Michigan," I offered.

"Sure. I have to figure out what to do with my bike, though."

"Oh, no worries. Bring it into the lobby. I'll see if Felix can keep an eye on it for a minute," I said.

"Felix?"

"Our doorman. He's super nice."

The older man met us at the door, decked out in his black suit and matching hat, his gray hair sticking out. "Good evening, Piper."

"Hi. Could my friend Wooyoung leave his bike here for a few?"

"Sure. Just lean it against the wall," he said.

"Thanks, we won't be long."

I led Wooyoung to the elevator, then pushed the button for my floor. The car jerked slightly, then began its short ascent. A few seconds later, we climbed out and headed down the hall. My apartment was near the end, so I only had a neighbor on one side, coincidentally, my ex. Nervousness washed over me as I unlocked my door and brought him inside. I'd never had a guy in here before. Today was definitely full of firsts.

"Here we are," I said.

"Wow, look at that view." Wooyoung made his way across the hardwood floors to peer out my French doors.

"I know. It's the main reason I got this place. I love listening to the waves at night once the traffic has slowed down. And the sunsets are beautiful. Even the storms are gorgeous when the water sorta crashes and gets all frothy."

"Can we go onto the deck?" he asked.

"Of course." I flushed, remembering my morning army crawl drill. I swung the door open, stepping outside. Already the wind licked at my skin, sending goosebumps over it.

"I could sit here for hours." He tipped his head back, staring at the lake.

Wooyoung and I leaned against the railing. Eyes closed, I enjoyed the familiar sounds around me, happy he could cherish a quiet moment with me.

Then came the most unpleasant noise in the world—the door from the deck next to mine opening.

"Piper," Minho called.

Damn it. Didn't he catch the hint I was avoiding him and didn't want to talk?

Without thinking, I reached over, grabbed hold of Wooyoung, and pulled him close to me, crushing my lips against his.

He seemed startled at first, but then his arms circled my waist, tugging me against his firm chest. His lips tasted of the after-dinner mint from the pub. They were soft and warm.

My pulse thundered in my ears as my mouth opened slightly, his tongue darting in, deepening the kiss. Everything inside me felt ablaze. As if, at any moment, I'd explode like a bomb on a battlefield.

My fingers tangled in his hair until a soft moan escaped my lips. Breathless, we pulled apart.

"I…"

"Shh, you don't have to say anything." His thumb grazed my bottom lip. This time, he leaned in, brushing his mouth against mine. "I'll see myself out. If you want, I can pick you up for work tomorrow. This time in my car."

"Okay."

He eased away, moving toward the door. "See you in the morning, Piper."

"Bye. And thank you."

"For what?" His eyes twinkled. "The kiss or dinner?"

"Both." My face burned.

He chuckled, then headed out.

"Did you have to do that right in front of me?" Minho said from the other deck.

I snorted, almost forgetting he'd been there. "Why should you care? Besides, I got to witness you fornicating with Hani in our car. So, I don't think we're quite even, do you? And if you really don't want to see what goes on over here, put up a wall or partition. Or better yet, move."

With that, I rushed inside, and fell backward onto the couch.

Holy crap. Wooyoung about incinerated me with that kiss.

I reached for my laptop bag and tugged out my computer. For the first time in a long time, I felt like writing.

Chapter Five

KERRIE

Juggling my purse on one shoulder and carrying Nella's overloaded backpack on my other, I pushed into our breezeway, which led to the kitchen. When I got to the center island, I dropped everything on the counter with a resounding thud.

"How much homework did they send home with you, Nella?" I wiped a bead of sweat from my forehead. I didn't remember Sophie having this much when she was in second grade.

"Only math and reading." Nella smiled at me, swinging her doll around.

Shit, what'd they do, send the Ten Commandment Tablets home with her? "Why's your bag so heavy?"

"Oh, Ms. Hollister let me bring home our pet rocks for the week. Mama, maybe later you can help me give them a bath."

Pet rocks? I guess it was better than a hamster or fish or something. "Honey, I don't think the rocks will need a bath."

She frowned. "They're not just rocks. They're *pet* rocks. So, we have to take care of them. Ms. Hollister says they need to eat dirt and be watered."

"Maybe Ms. Hollister needs to eat dirt," I muttered, allowing a heavy sigh to escape my lips. What in God's name were they being taught? "Maybe later. Let's get you a snack."

I still had to get laundry done if I wanted to avoid any more bathroom mishaps. My body was already begging to be set free from the organ constricting skirt. At this rate, I'd be lucky not to have internal bleeding, or at the very least, a collapsed spleen, if that was even a thing.

With another sigh, I glanced at the fridge, realizing I'd forgotten to take something out for dinner. Unless Hal had. His truck was parked in the front when I came in, but I knew better than to count on him actually being helpful.

Taking two packs of fruit snacks from the cupboard, I got the kids situated at the counter on barstools, when a low moaning sound came from down the hall.

Tommy's eyes got big. "Mommy, I...I think there's a ghost in the house."

"I'm sure it's nothing." My face reddened. *Damn it, Hal.* He knew the kids would be home soon.

"No, I hear it, too. Maybe we should check it out." Nella scooted from her seat, then went to the utensil drawer to grab a large carving knife.

"Give me that." I took the weapon from Nella and put it back where it'd come from. "Um, you two stay here. I'll go instead. In case it's something big and scary." I put my hands up, pretending to lunge at them.

They screamed, then started laughing.

My fists clenched at my side as I trudged down the hall to our bedroom. Irritation radiated through me as I pounded on the door. "Hal, the kids and I are home. Keep the TV down."

Of course, I knew it wasn't the TV. It was whichever flavor of the week he'd snuck into the house.

The noises stopped on the other side of the door, and I backed away. I hated this. How much more could I endure? I had a few thousand saved up, but I'd need a deposit, not to mention the first month's rent, plus money to get utilities started. And I'd have to buy some things for the house. I planned on taking most of the kids' stuff from here when I finally left, but I'd need dishes, furniture, linens. Just thinking about it made me stressed.

Perhaps I should've asked for alimony or something, at least until I got settled. Piper had indicated Hal would have to buy me out if he kept the house. She said her mother had been through enough divorces that she had the basic knowledge down pat. Soon, I'd broach the subject with my ex.

When I got back to the kitchen, I caught sight of a blonde woman scurrying across my driveway and through my front yard, tugging on her shoes. Crap.

"Ugh, who wants to play a quick game of find the cereal?" I asked, grabbing a box of Frosty O's from the cupboard. I took a couple handfuls out and tossed them on the floor. "Whoever picks up the most will get a dollar."

The kids leapt down from their chairs and raced across the kitchen. *Please let this keep them distracted.* Just then, Hal emerged from the room, tucking his shirt in, and stepping on several pieces of cereal.

"What the hell happened out here?" His coffee-colored eyes met mine. His sandy hair was tousled, his skin flushed.

My jaw clenched. "You're kidding me, right? I had to distract them so they didn't see the person running across our yard, putting clothes on. You say you want to keep this a secret? Well, it's hard to do when you're banging a blonde a day while the kids are here. I'm literally over this. I can't keep up the charade."

His brow furrowed. "You're blaming me for cereal on the floor? Does that even make sense?"

"Yes, it does, you...you asshole." I lowered my voice to a loud whisper. "Jesus, Hal, I'm trying to parent our kids. And you're not helping."

"Look, we made a deal. You keep this quiet for a bit longer, and you can stay here. No bills. No worries."

No worries. Right. He obviously didn't get it. My chest tightened as I bit back the urge to cry. We might be divorced, but I was still human, for hell's sake.

The side door burst open, and Sophie came in. "We might need to call the cops. I saw some woman trying to break in or something. She was by the window when Mya first pulled up to drop me off."

Hal's face turned a nice shade of tomato.

"Crap. Hal, maybe you should call," I urged.

"I'm sure it was nothing." He glowered at me.

"She was by the window. She could be a peeping Tom or Jane or whatever you call a female version." My lips quivered as I tried to keep from smiling. That's right, let him have to deal with this for once.

"Dad, seriously, I'm not lying," Sophie implored, her brown eyes narrowed.

"Okay, I'll go check things out. I don't think we need to call the cops." He shoved his work boots on and trudged outside as though he was really concerned for our safety.

The kids all moved to the side window to watch him "investigate." Hal walked around the house, pretending to examine things. A few minutes later, he came back in. "Whoever was there is gone. We'll just keep a closer eye on things and lock the doors."

Sophie rolled her eyes. "The lady looked super trashy, like maybe she was a druggie or something. But, oh well, hopefully we don't get murdered in our sleep tonight."

I could've kissed Sophie right then. Ha, wonder what Hal thought about his newest fling being compared to a druggie?

"I don't want to die," Nella said, her face scrunching.

"You're not going to die, now stop. Why don't you and your brother finish picking up the cereal, then ask Daddy for a dollar." My gaze met Hal's. "Satisfied?"

"It won't happen again," he said. "I'll be out of town for a few days. I'll text you when I'm coming back."

Of course, he would. Tears pricked my eyes as I went into my room to grab the overflowing laundry hamper. "Just another couple of months. You can do this."

Whether Hal wanted people to know about our divorce or not, I wasn't going to keep playing games. At some point, he'd have to grow a pair and tell his family he'd fucked up.

Literally.

Chapter Six

MAUDE

My gaze flicked to my watch again. Corny was late. Not just a few minutes late, but a half an hour. He'd probably fallen asleep on the couch watching those damned soap operas. He'd taken a liking to them when he retired.

He knew which family had an illegitimate child trying to steal the dead father's fortune, which brother stole the other's wife, and all those nonsense plotlines. If I had one of those cellular phones, I'd call him.

From the corner of my eye, I noticed Mr. Dancy leaving the building. He was always the last one out. Mainly because he liked to shut off all the air conditioning/heat before he left at night.

With a sigh, I hurried toward him, trying not to catch my heel in the crack of the sidewalk.

"Mr. Dancy!"

"Maude. What are you still doing here?" He glanced around the nearly empty lot, the late day sun reflecting off his head.

"I think Cornelius fell asleep or something. Would you mind letting me back in to call him?"

"Sure. If you need a ride, let me know."

I followed him back into the building, trying to ignore the strong scent of his spicy cologne. Phew, the man must've bathed in it. We went to the main desk in the front lobby, and I dialed Nine to get an outside line. Our number rang and rang before the answering machine picked up.

"Corny, are you there? You forgot to pick me up. You better not be napping or getting into the ice cream, or so help me."

I hung up, then waited a few minutes and tried again. But the answering machine picked up for the second time. Either he was on his way, or he really had fallen asleep. Should I wait here a little longer? Or take Mr. Dancy up on his offer?

I hesitated only a few more minutes, then turned back to my boss. "I suppose I'll take you up on that offer to bring me home. It'll serve Corny right if he has to drive all the way here and find me gone."

Clutching my purse to my side, I followed Mr. Dancy back outside into the stifling heat and to his circa 1970s boat of a car, painted in a deep olive shade. Or what I like to call baby-poo-green. When he unlocked the doors, the stench of stale cigar smoke clung to the air. I waved my hand in front of my face.

"Sorry about that. Miriam doesn't let me smoke them in the house, so I have to do it in the car on my way home from work."

"I can see why, they stink to high heaven," I said.

"You sound just like her."

"Smart woman, then." I smiled, sliding across the faux leather seats, which were hot against my legs. At this rate, it'd be warm enough to iron out the wrinkles in my skin.

After surviving the rush hour traffic, we pulled up to my house. I noticed the car was gone. I frowned. Had Corny went to get me? "Thanks for the ride. Do you want some gas money or something?"

"If you have a few dollars, I'd appreciate it. Gas is expensive these days."

Of course, he'd want some. Mr. Frugal, indeed. I slipped my wallet from my purse and handed him a ten. Sweet Jesus, he'd probably charge me tax if he could.

"I'll be driving back past the office, so if I see Cornelius out there, I'll let him know you're home safe."

"That'd be appreciated."

"Alright then, I'll see you tomorrow."

I shut the door, and he backed out of my driveway, nearly taking down my mailbox in the process.

Groaning, I hurried up the sidewalk. I twisted the knob on the door to find it unlocked. First Corny didn't pick me up, then he left the door unlocked for intruders to walk in. He and I were going to have a serious talk tonight. He'd be lucky if I made dinner at this rate.

I set my things on the counter, knocking over some of Corny's medicine bottles in the process. Noticing the red message indicator blinking on the answering machine, I went over to check it. There were three messages. I hit Play. "Hi Maude, this is Peggy from Doctor Fleming's office. I didn't have your work phone, but there's been an emergency and we're trying to reach you. Cornelius was transported to the hospital this afternoon. I will try to contact you again in a little bit."

The second message was from me, and the third was from Doctor Fleming's office again. With a hiss of air and shaky hands, I picked up the cordless phone and dialed Peggy. I wondered if she was still there. It was after hours now. Panic clutched my airway.

The line went directly to voicemail, which gave the hours of operation. I considered calling the hospital, but instead I grabbed the spare car keys, threw them in my purse, and hurried to the door. They likely wouldn't tell me anything over the phone, anyway, might as well just go to the hospital.

My stomach knotted. What was going on? Was it a true emergency? This wasn't the first time I'd gotten a call like this. It was just like Corny to wait until something got bad enough and needed to go to the ER instead of taking care of it early on. The man was so damn stubborn.

Crossing my yard, I made my way over to Griff's house, one of Corny's close friends and our long-time neighbor. He'd been widowed for fifteen years now and liked to stop in and play a few hands of cards with my husband. But he was a sly one, that Griff was. He flirted like I was a retired Hugh Heffner Bunny.

When I got to his front door, which was painted an obnoxious shade of yellow, I knocked. The door swung open, and Griff stood eyeing me. His thinning hair was sticking up in unruly tufts, his white whiskers in need of a good shaving. "Maude, darling, to what do I owe this pleasure?"

I snorted. "Listen, this is a business visit. I wondered if you could take me down to the hospital.? Corny had the car today and they've sent him to the ER."

He raised an eyebrow. "Anything serious?"

"No. I don't know, perhaps. Can you give me a ride or not? Corny's gonna have a lot to answer for when I get there."

"Hmm...is there trouble in paradise?" He waggled his eyebrows at me.

"Griff, do you want me to take my shoe off and swat you one? Quit being a twit. Can you drive me or not?"

"Yeah, yeah. Just let me get my keys. Ungrateful woman," he muttered under his breath.

When he came outside, he opened the door to his white Cadillac for me. Unlike Mr. Dancy's car, his smelled like the pine air-freshener hanging from his mirror. At least he kept it clean.

It took us about twenty minutes to get through traffic. Soon, we parked in the lot for the emergency room.

"Thanks for the lift, Griff. I'll make some cookies for you later this week as repayment."

He waved it off. "The only sweets I need, darling, are your smiles."

"Wait until I tell Corny you're coming onto me. He'll punch you good and hard in the mouth."

Griff laughed. "Are you sure you don't want me to stick around? You and Corny might need a ride home. Or if you've got spare keys, I can always have one of the boys head over with me and get your car dropped off at the hospital for you."

"Well, if you're offering, that'd be helpful." I dug into my purse until I found the keys, then handed them to Griff. "You can leave these in the glove box with the door unlocked once you get back here. Thanks again."

"No problem. See you around, Maude."

I slammed the door shut and gave a quick wave before heading inside. The sterile scent I always associated with hospitals hung heavy in the air. A small child cried while their mother rocked them back and forth in one of the waiting room chairs, making soothing noises.

Moving to the ER check-in window, a brown-haired man smiled at me from the other side of the glass.

"Hi, how can I help you tonight?"

"My husband Cornelius Gilchrist was brought in earlier," I said into the small round hole, as I leaned on the counter. "I'm his wife, Maude Gilcrhist."

His smile faltered. "Of course, why don't you have a seat. Someone will be right out in a moment."

My wrinkled fingers clutched my purse tight to my chest. I swallowed hard, trying not to let my imagination run wild. After all, Corny had been in the hospital numerous times over the years for trivial things.

After a while, the doors near the front window slung open slowly and a doctor in blue scrubs stepped out, along with our family practitioner, Dr. Fleming.

"Mrs. Gilchrist?" The one in scrubs called me over. "I'm Dr. Baxter. Could you come on back for a moment?"

Climbing from my seat, I gathered my things and joined them. "Sure, how's Corny? Is everything okay?"

"We'll explain everything when we get back in one of the rooms."

After swiping his badge, Dr. Baxter ushered myself and Dr. Fleming through the automatic doors. My heels clicked against the polished floors while the sounds of machines whirring and beeping hummed around us.

We entered a small examination type room where Dr. Baxter motioned for me to sit.

"Tom...I mean, I mean Dr. Fleming?" I turned to our family physician first.

His eyes seemed glassy as he sat beside me, reached for my hand, and gave it a squeeze. Tom had known Corny and I for twenty-five years. He'd taken over his father, Simon's, practice years ago.

"Mrs. Gilchrist, I'm sorry to have to deliver this news, but your husband had a ruptured aneurysm earlier today."

My jaw dropped as I stared at him.

Tom cleared his throat, still holding my hand. "It was a significant brain bleed. He collapsed in our office. We immediately called EMS, and he was rushed to the hospital."

"W-what are you saying?" I glanced between them, trembling. "He's okay, right?"

Tom shook his head while Dr. Baxter continued. "Unfortunately, Cornelius passed away enroute to the ER. We attempted to resuscitate him, but it was too late. I'm truly sorry."

"No, this can't be. How did this happen? He was on medication..."

"Maude, I don't know if he was actually taking it." Tom released my fingers. "And even if he was, sometimes these things can still happen."

Dr. Baxter went over to the counter and retrieved a plastic bag. He handed it to me. "These are your husband's personal effects."

My heart thundered against my chest like a train barreling at full speed. Peering inside, I found Corny's watch, his wedding ring, wallet, and our car keys.

"H-he's gone?" My mouth formed the question as if saying it out loud would somehow change things.

"Yes, Maude," Tom whispered beside me.

"Cornelius already had a funeral home listed in some of his paperwork. Dilly & Sons. Is this where you still want his body to go?" Dr. Baxter asked.

Numb, I nodded. What more could I do?

Corny was gone. *Gone.*

Dr. Baxter said more words I didn't hear, but I nodded as if I did. Pulling the keys from the bag, my fist tightened around them, cutting into my hand. "I-I think I've heard enough. I'm ready to go now." I stood suddenly.

"Are you sure you're okay to drive home?" Tom climbed to his feet, as well. "I can drop you off."

"No, I'm fine. I'll be fine."

When I got to the parking lot, my car was there, just as Griff promised. Before climbing in, I leaned against the door, a sob escaping my lips. This wasn't happening. There had to be a mistake.

Fifty years of marriage, and he just leaves me like this. No goodbye, no heads up. Just poof, gone?

Had Cornelius known something was wrong this morning? He'd been pushing me to drive. That son of beehive.

"When I see him again, I'm going to throttle him." I shook my hand at the sky.

My legs trembled beneath me as anger rushed through. How could he do this to me? Was nothing sacred anymore?

I had to keep it together. I had to. No amount of crying would fix this.

At last, I slid into the car, and tears flooded my cheeks. I cried until nothing was left in me. Then, I pounded the steering wheel until I thought it might actually break off.

Long minutes passed before I finally put the keys in the ignition and drove home. I didn't remember much about the drive. Trudging inside, I dropped mine and Corny's belongings on the table, my eyes landing on the bottles of pills on the counter. The ones I'd knocked over earlier.

Taking a deep breath, I moved to pick them up. There were pills for his heart and cholesterol, as well as for his blood pressure. My eye caught the date on them. They were from eight months ago. Fingers shaking, I pried open several bottles to find them mostly full.

He hadn't been taking them, just as Dr. Fleming assumed.

"You bastard, Cornelius Gilchrist. You lying, treacherous leech. The girls were right, men are shits. They're complete and utter shits. You could've prevented this."

Chapter Seven

PIPER

Nervousness clenched hold of me as I stood in the lobby the next morning, waiting for Wooyoung to pick me up. What if he changed his mind about me after the kiss? I'd practically thrown myself at him like a dog in heat.

"Piper, hey." Minho came up alongside me. "Listen, I wish you'd stop avoiding me and talk to me."

I froze. No. No. No. Not again this morning. Why couldn't he just leave me alone? He obviously had no idea how much his affair had destroyed me.

Biting back the lump in my throat, I spun to face him, trying to paste a smile on my face. "There's nothing to say. Your actions spoke loud enough when you decided to sleep with someone who wasn't me."

He frowned. "I'm sorry, I never meant to hurt you. The truth is, I miss you."

"Say what?" My hand tightened around the strap of my purse. What the hell was he on about?

"Not in the sense of us being a couple, but I miss having you as a friend. For God's sake, you've been my friend since elementary school."

"You should've thought about that before. I...I can't be friends with you. Why can't you understand that?" My eyes welled. Where was Wooyoung? Damnit it, I needed to get out of here. "I loved you, Minho. From the moment we first meant, there's only been you. You can't expect me to jump on board with this...whatever it is you're trying to do."

His brow furrowed. He actually had the audacity to look hurt by my answer. "Piper, please..."

"Nope. Sorry, I'm not in the right mind frame to forgive and be friends." Hurrying toward the front door, I moved away from him and to the sidewalk out front of our apartment building. Right then, Wooyoung pulled up, and I let out a sigh of relief.

He parked, then hopped from his car to get the door for me.

"Think about it, Piper," Minho hollered after me.

And like any rational human being, I flipped him the bird and slid into the vehicle, the cream-colored leather seats cool against my legs.

When Wooyoung climbed in, he peered over at me. "Are you okay?"

"I...yeah. I'm just so freaking pissed right now. Minho had the nerve to ask if we could still be friends. After he literally ruined my life. I just can't with that man. Does he not get it?"

"What a prick! I'm sorry he keeps bothering you. Maybe in time, you won't think about him anymore and you'll be able to move on. I mean, I know a pretty great guy who has a thing for you." He grinned at me.

My gaze met his as I remembered our kiss again. Cheeks on fire, I smiled. "Hmm. Perhaps, you'll be the one to help me move on."

He reached over and swiped a strand of my auburn hair from my face. "I'd like that. So, no more worries about your ex. He never deserved you, Piper."

My eyes focused on his lips, my heart skittering against my chest like someone skipping a stone across water. He leaned in, the scent of mint on his breath, his hand cupping my chin.

A horn blared behind us, and we jumped apart.

"Guess, I should get moving. This isn't a real parking spot." Wooyoung's cheeks pinkened, making him even more adorable. "Oh, before I forget, I stopped and grabbed you a coffee on my way over."

I glanced at the drink holder between us. The cup had my name in all caps with hearts drawn around it. "Thanks. Did you request the drawing on this, as well?"

My mouth turned up at the corners as his blush deepened. "Um, not exactly. The barista took it upon herself to help me make a good impression."

With a laugh, I took a sip. "I appreciate the pick-me-up. One of these days, I'll repay you."

He side-eyed me from the driver's seat. "No. You don't have to. I like doing things for you."

This time, I blushed. Geez, what was I, thirteen? Butterflies fluttered in my belly. This was so new. It'd been a long time since I'd felt flutters like this. Actually, if I was being honest with myself, I'd never had flutters like this with Minho. Was it because we'd grown up together, and had just kind of stepped into coupledom? Either way, maybe this is what it was supposed to feel like, falling for someone, I mean.

When we pulled up to work, Wooyoung and I parted ways, and I headed straight to Mr. Dancy's office. He peered up from his desk.

"Piper, what can I do for you?"

I handed him the greeting card idea I'd typed up the night before. My teeth grazed my lip as he read it.

He slammed his hand down on his desk, nearly giving me a heart attack. "Yes! This is what I've been waiting for. I knew you could do it, kid! Did Maude talk to you?" He slid my idea into his folder.

A wooden frame holding a photo of him, his wife, and three sons sat in the middle of his desk, along with three signed golf balls in small glass display boxes. I had no idea whose signatures they were, but they'd been there since before I'd started.

"No, I, uh...I had a breakthrough last night." If you counted a very smoldering kiss as a breakthrough. My heart raced at the thought of our passionate exchange.

It's not like I could tell Mr. Dancy that Wooyoung's lips were my muse.

"Good, good. Well, wherever this spark came from, embrace it, Piper. This is good."

I'd like to do more than embrace it, but that wasn't a tale I'd tell my boss.

My shoulders grew lighter as I left his office and went to mine. I waved to Kerrie on the way through. "See you at lunch."

"Yes, I want details about dinner last night, woman."

"Yeah, yeah. Of course, you do."

"I'm living vicariously through you," she said, her dark hair falling into her face.

"Where's Maude?" I noticed her dark office. She was always here before us.

"Not sure. Mr. Dancy said she was taking a few days off. Maybe she finally decided to quit showing us up and actually use some of her vacation time."

"Not likely."

I worked on a new card. The ideas were definitely flowing better. When lunch arrived, I went to the cafeteria and found Kerrie waiting for me, her peanut butter sandwich nearly gone.

"So?" She quirked an eyebrow.

My gaze shifted to where Wooyoung sat with a few of the guys from HR. "Dinner was great. We really hit it off."

"And?"

I laughed. "You assume there's more."

"Since your face is practically crimson, yes, I do."

"We kissed," I blurted. "And it was amazing. Like, rock your world, light you on fire, kind of heat."

"That's awesome. I'm so happy for you!" Kerrie grabbed her bottle of water and chugged it.

My eyes met Wooyoung's, and he waved at me. I waved back.

"But maybe this isn't a good idea. We work together. What if something goes wrong? I'll have to see him every day."

"Oh no, you don't. Don't you dare psych yourself out. He's not Minho."

Sighing, I twisted the top off my diet cola. "I know. It's just hard. And speaking of Minho, he cornered me in the lobby today, told me he missed me, and wants us to be friends."

"You're kidding, right?"

"No. I wish I was. He's such an asshole. He can't seem to get the hint that what he did fucking sucked."

My cell buzzed in my pocket. "Oh, I should take this really quick. It's my stepdad, David." Or rather, ex-stepfather. Out of all the men my mother had been married to, he was my favorite. My bio dad had died when I was so young, sometimes I had a hard time remembering him. David, though, had been there through my awkward years when I was on the cusp of becoming a teenager.

Mom was part of the reason I had so many trust and relationship issues. I desperately wanted to find the love of my life and be married forever. Which was what I thought I'd had with Minho. But, as Mom liked to point out, most high school sweethearts don't make it.

"David, hey."

"How's my favorite daughter?"

"Doing okay. And you?"

"Pretty good. I was calling to let you know I'm back in town, so if you'd like to meet up for dinner or lunch one of these days, I'd love to see you, kiddo."

Kiddo. Hah. David never seemed to realize I'd aged.

"Sounds perfect. I'll let you know when I'm free. Have you talked to Mom lately?"

"No. Last I heard, she'd gone to Spain with, what's-his-name. The new husband."

I laughed. "I don't even keep track anymore. By the time I get used to one being around, she's on to the next. You're the only one I've ever considered my dad, and the only one I keep tabs on."

"I'm glad. Your mom isn't all bad, Piper. I obviously fell in love with her for a reason."

"I know, but still."

"Well, I know you're on your lunch hour, so I won't keep you. Talk to you soon."

"Okay. Love you."

"Love you, too. Take care, Piper."

Kerrie and I spent the rest of the lunch hour dissecting the kiss I'd shared with Wooyoung. She encouraged me to pursue whatever this was going on between us to see where it went.

Fear coiled in my stomach, but I knew I couldn't hide away forever. There was something between Wooyoung and I. Didn't it deserve to be tested and given a chance?

Chapter Eight
KERRIE

Nella sat next to me at the center island, her shadow box between us. Her blonde hair stuck to her face, where I was pretty sure she'd gotten glitter glue. She was in charge of making the grass out of thinly cut pieces of construction paper, while I helped make the animals.

I rolled brown clay between my hands to make the body of the dog, then grabbed two tiny balls of clay for the front legs before moving to make the back ones.

"Ew, that looks like a wiener," Tommy said, laughing as he poked his head up next to me to watch.

My oldest, Sophie, laughed as she made her way across the kitchen. "He's right. It kind of looks like a wiener, Mom."

"Because I don't have the back legs on yet. Just give it a second." I hurried to make more legs. After I stuck them on, I turned to the kids. "See, no more wiener."

"Er...you should definitely add the head and ears, because now it just looks like a deformed one." Sophie laughed. "Maybe I should help Nella instead."

With a sigh, I stood. "Have at it. And by the way, how do you know what boy parts look like, anyway?"

"The internet, Mom. Everything is on the internet."

"Christ."

"Totally kidding. I've had sex ed at school, and I changed Tommy's diapers when he was little."

"What's sex ed?" Nella asked.

My face burned as I turned to glance at Sophie. "Nothing you need to worry about for a few more years."

"How come I always have to wait a few more years?" Nella stuck her lip out.

"Because that's what we have to do as kids," Sophie said. She helped finish the rest of the animals, thankfully making sure no more resembled the male anatomy.

The side door opened, and Hal came inside. He immediately headed toward the living room. "Tommy, can you grab Daddy a pop?"

"Yeah."

"Don't shake it this time," Hal hollered. "What's for dinner?"

Was he kidding me right now? Fuming, I tried to keep the malice from my voice. "Haven't gotten a chance to start it yet. I had to help the kids with homework."

"Alright, let me know when you get it going."

If the kids weren't standing right here, I'd have told him to shove it and make his own food.

"Sure."

"Hey, Mom?" Sophie said, as I walked over to check the cupboards and fridge for an easy dinner option.

"Yeah?"

"Do you have a cami I can borrow to go under my light blue shirt for tomorrow?"

"I should have a clean one in my top left-hand drawer. There's a white one and a black one."

"Thanks."

Sophie disappeared down the hall while Nella and Tommy went to the living room with Hal. I grabbed a box of noodles from the lazy-Susan, along with a can of marinara sauce. Hopefully, I still had some Italian sausage left.

Not more than a minute had gone by when Sophie stormed into the kitchen.

"What is this?" She shoved a packet of papers at me. "I found them in your underwear drawer. Is this for real? Are you guys really divorced?"

Crap. I read the header: Judgment of Divorce. "Look, I...I can explain."

Her eyes narrowed. "Why are we living here if he divorced you? I'm not stupid, I've seen him traipsing women in here when he thinks we're not looking or not home or whatever. At first, I thought he was having affairs and you were okay with it. But now..."

"It's complicated. Look, your dad decided he didn't want to be together, but I can't afford to move yet."

"Do Grandma and Grandpa know? Does anyone know?" Her hand was shaking as she shoved the papers at me.

"No, he didn't want your grandparents to know or you kids. H-he didn't want to be the bad guy."

"Well, he is. He's a fucking dick." Sophie's voice cracked. "And you're letting him walk all over you. You deserve better than this. Even if you make me mad sometimes, at least you're always here when I need you."

"Is everything okay in there?" Hal called.

Sophie opened her mouth to say something, but I quickly intervened. "Sophie and I are going to for a drive. So, you'll have to get dinner for you and the kids." I folded the papers and tucked them into my purse.

"I just got home from work," Hal argued.

"So did Mom," Sophie snapped back.

"We'll be home later." I didn't wait for him to respond again. Instead, I grabbed the keys to the minivan, and we hurried to the driveway.

"Can I drive?" Sophie asked.

"Are you sure you're okay to drive?" She only had her permit. I'd been trying to get her more hours in so we could finally get her license. Not that there wasn't a lot of public transit options, but we still wanted her to be able to drive. With me working now, I didn't have as much time to take her out. And asking Hal seemed to always be out of the question.

"I-I'll be fine."

I handed over the keys and followed her to the van. She climbed into the driver's seat and adjusted it for her longer legs while I climbed into the passenger side. Once we both had our seatbelts on, Sophie adjusted her mirrors.

"When did Dad file?" She broke the silence as soon as we pulled out of the driveway.

"Last year. Because I was agreeable to everything, it was done pretty quickly."

"I don't understand why you didn't say anything."

Tears welled in my eyes. "Because I was embarrassed. Still am. No one knows half of what's happened or is still happening."

"We should move, Mom. Seriously, you aren't his maid or whatever. He treats you like shit."

"Language."

"Well, it's true."

"I know, but he's still your dad."

She snorted. "Hardly, he never does anything with us anymore. It's like his body was taken hostage by an alien."

I laughed. "True. Listen, I only need another couple of months to have the money I'll need for everything. Turn right at the stop sign."

She signaled and turned.

We kept driving for another couple of blocks.

"Take a left at the light," I said.

Traffic whirred by us on the right and left. Sophie's hands tightened on the wheel. When she had a clearing, she quickly maneuvered us onto the next road. Just then, red and blue lights flashed behind us.

"Oh, crap. What do I do?" Sophie freaked, taking her eyes off the road.

"Ah, first, watch where you're going. Secondly, pull off into that parking lot there." I pointed to the grocery store lot on my side.

We sat there for several minutes when an officer came to Sophie's window. She rolled it down. "Mr. Walker?"

"Sophie, how's it going?" he asked.

"Better about ten minutes ago," she muttered. "Don't tell Mya you pulled me over."

He chuckled, revealing perfect, shiny white teeth. His rich brown skin was smooth, except for the laugh lines around his eyes. His dark hair was cut short against his head. His broad shoulders seemed to fill the window.

I gulped a deep breath. Holy, hot damn, he was good looking. And apparently, Sophie's best friend's dad. How had I missed this before?

I quickly smoothed my hair and attempted to smile.

"Do you know why I pulled you over?"

Sophie shook her head.

"You forgot to signal at the light, and you also have a taillight out. I'll need to see your license and registration."

"She only has her permit," I said.

"Mrs. Holloway, good to see you."

"That's Ms. Holloway now," Sophie corrected.

"Soph—"

"Oh, my bad. I didn't realize you were divorced."

I nodded, then reached to open the glove box to get the registration. A large pink vibrator fell into my lap.

Sophie's eyes widened, and Officer Walker swiftly turned away, but not before I caught a smirk on his face.

Oh, God. No. I'd forgotten I'd thrown it there after the whole lightsaber, kid-getting-smacked-in-the-face-with-it thing. My cheeks were on fire. "Um, this is my ex-husband's van. I have no idea why that would be in there."

"Mom," Sophie shrieked.

Officer Walker chuckled. "If that's the worst thing I see fall out of a glove box today, I'll call it a good one."

Fishing for the registration, I handed it across to him.

"I'll just check a few things and be back." He walked to his patrol car.

"Mom, I swear, I've never been more mortified in my life."

"That makes two of us," I hissed. "It's not like I purposely pulled it and waved it around like Harry Potter with his wand."

"Bad imagery, Mom." She groaned, shaking her head. "J-just get rid of that thing."

I moved to put it in my purse. "Fine, out of sight, out of mind."

"Mom, seriously, you can't put it there. What if Nella or Tommy find it?"

I didn't have the heart to tell her that's how it'd originally ended up in the glove box to begin with.

"Well, what do you want me to do with it? I can't just toss it out the window. Then we'll get a ticket for littering, or I might hit someone with it and get charged with assault and battery."

Sophie cringed. "Alight, just put it back in the glove box for now and throw it away or whatever when we get home."

When Officer Walker came back, he handed us our paperwork. "Okay, I'll let you go without a ticket this time. Make sure to get the taillight fixed, and Sophie, you need to use your signals. I don't want this to mar you being able to get your license."

"Thank you, Officer Walker," I said.

"Demarcus," he said. "You can call me Demarcus. Our girls have been friends a long time, so I don't think we need the formalities."

"Demarcus." His name rolled off my tongue like butter. My insides coiled with heat. It'd been a long time since I'd been with someone, and my body was signaling to me.

"I'll see you around."

When he left, Sophie switched seats. "So, today will forever be known as Dildo-Divorce-Gate."

"What?"

"You know, kind of like Watergate or Deflate Gate, but only with dildos and divorce news."

I laughed. "Alright, then. But let's not mention Dildo-Divorce-Gate again. Kind of want to leave this moment behind us. In fact, how about we head home now?"

"Okay."

"Sophie, can you please keep this quiet from your siblings for now? We can tell them when we get ready to move. And I sorta promised your dad not to tell Grandma and Grandpa."

"Fine. But I'm not going to keep quiet about this forever," she said.

"I don't expect you to."

"Can I at least talk to Mya? She's been through this before when her mom and dad divorced."

"That's fine."

"I love you, Mom."

"I love you, too."

A part of me felt relieved to have her know. At least it was one less person I had to lie to.

"So, I'm not sure if this is the best time to bring this up or not, but my birthday is coming up. Obviously, you know that," Sophie said. "And I wondered if you might get me tickets to a concert coming to town? You could go with me. Mya and her mom were planning on attending. They just released more tickets. I think they're planning on getting a hotel room, too."

"Well, it is your seventeenth birthday, your last year before turning into an adult. Why don't you send me a link with the information, and I'll talk with your dad about watching the kids so we can go." Maybe I could get Hal to pay for it, too, so it wouldn't come out of my savings. Not that it mattered. I wanted Sophie's day to be special, even if it meant a couple extra weeks under the same roof as my ex.

Later that night, after I tucked the youngest two in, I walked past Sophie's room to hear her on the phone.

"Yeah, I just found out today about my parents' divorce. It really sucks. I was mad at first, but now, I just want Mom to be happy and to stand up to my dad. He's seriously an asshole. She didn't really state the reasons for the divorce, but she didn't really have to. I know he's had affairs. She deserves better than him."

Tears slid down my cheeks. She was right, I did deserve better, and hopefully soon, I'd be able to move on.

Chapter Nine

MAUDE

Rubbing the sleep from my eyes, I reached across my bed. *Empty.*

I fisted some of the blue quilt in my hand, staring at Corny's pillow. Hellfire. Two weeks he'd been gone. The house was quiet, save for the scratching sound of the tree branch against the siding outside my window. How could he do this to me? This question had pounded in my head every night since he'd left. Fifty years of marriage. Gone. Snuffed like a candle left out in a rainstorm..

I'd been on the phone with my lawyer, going through paperwork and bills, and making phone calls. It was never ending. Tears burned at the back of my eyes, and I raised my fingers to brush them away. I didn't know what to feel anymore. Angry? Sad? Frustrated? So many emotions swirled through me. Was there a right way to do this?

Tossing back my covers, I slid from bed, putting on my fuzzy red slippers. Today, I'd force myself to go back to work. If I kept busy, I wouldn't have time to focus on Corny's *betrayal*. Nor would I have time to rehash every conversation we'd had over the last six months to see if I'd missed some sort of clue. But other than him pushing for me to drive again, there'd been nothing.

He'd acted the same. Every morning, breakfast together, lunch at my work in the afternoon, then he'd pick me up, we'd come home, watch the news on television, read the funnies in the paper, and start all over again the next day. *If he'd only taken his damn medication.* How did I miss him not doing it? Why hadn't I paid closer attention?

I swallowed past the lump in my throat. No. I couldn't wallow in pity and sorrow. If nothing else, I had to be strong. Show Corny I'd be just fine without his wrinkled hind end. Besides, why should I blame myself for something he chose not to do?

"Asshole," I muttered to myself.

After a shower and a quick breakfast of toast and jam, I got ready for work. A pair of black slacks with matching jacket, and a red and white polka-dotted shirt, which tied at the neck underneath.

Once I finished dressing, I searched the pantry for my old lunch box, and readied my food for the day. I had to get out the door sooner now that I'd be driving. Although, I suppose I could easily take the L Train. There was a stop not too far from the house. But I hated the idea of public transportation. Especially by myself. No. I'd make myself drive. It's not like I didn't know how. I was always just more comfortable with Corny doing it.

Corny. No. I wasn't going to think about him anymore today. I was the new and improved Maude now. Tough. Strong. Still having to wear my extra support bra.

Lunch in hand, I made my way outside, locking the front door behind me. It took me thirty minutes of white knuckled driving to get to work. I'd only been flipped off twice, so it was a good day.

When I got to my office, Mr. Dancy came sauntering toward me, and followed me inside.

"Maude, you're back? I thought you might want another week or two?" He didn't wait for me to ask him to take a seat, he just plopped in the chair on the other side of my desk.

"Ah, I need to stay busy. There's nothing more for me to do at home. The quietness is driving me crazy. Besides, the more I'm there, the angrier I get about what Corny did. Bloody bastard, anyway."

Mr. Dancy's eyes widened. "Well alright then. Welcome back."

He scurried out of the way, and back to his office. That was one way to get rid of him, make him uncomfortable. I chuckled to myself.

I flipped the button on my computer to get it up and running while I sorted through the stack of ideas I'd left in the basket on my desk. A picture of Corny and I at our fortieth wedding anniversary stared back at me.

My stomach knotted like a ball of yarn. Reaching forward, I flipped it face down. Biting back tears, I grabbed a tissue and dabbed my eyes. Without a second thought, I picked up the framed photograph and shoved it in my bottom drawer, out of sight.

For three hours, I attempted to come up with words of love. But I couldn't write anything. Damn, Corny. If our marriage could end like this, then how was I supposed to convince some poor sucker that love was forever? More like men were shits. Love didn't truly exist—only in movies, but not in real life.

My clock clicked over to noon, and I went and grabbed my lunch from the breakroom fridge, then trudged to find a place to sit in the cafeteria.

Wooyoung waved, then made his way toward me. "Hey, Maude. How are you? Is everything okay? I really missed seeing you."

I snorted. "Sure you did, kid. Sorry, not in the mood to chat at the moment."

"Oh, um, okay. I was just going to fill you in on the Piper front."

I held my hand up. "Let's not talk about it today. Maybe I'll feel better tomorrow."

He nodded, casting me several strange looks.

Instead, I made my way over to where Piper and Kerrie sat, their lunches already spread in front of them.

"Mind if I join you?" I asked.

Piper peered up. "No, of course not. But aren't you having lunch with your husband?"

I let out another snort. If I kept this up, I'd turn into a pig. "I might as well get this over with now, so you can say 'I told you so.' The two of you were right. Love does not exist. Men are jerks and bastards and every curse word under the sun. Corny left me. That no good, lying ass of a man is gone."

Kerrie's mouth dropped open. "Oh, God. Maude, I'm so sorry. Christ. How the hell could he walk away from you? You've been married forever."

"Exactly." I plopped next to them. "Fifty years I gave that man. And for him to do this to me. I want to wring his neck or run over his clothes with the lawn mower. Something to make me feel better." I opened my lunch box and pulled out a piece of chicken and some leftover potato salad I'd bought at the grocery store.

"You're better off without him," Piper said, holding up her iced tea.

Carlos, who was at the table beside ours, scooted his chair closer to us, and said, "Men are horrible jerks."

I frowned. "No men allowed at this table today."

Carlos smoothed his dark hair with his hand, his coffee-colored eyes catching mine. "How can you say that? I was wronged by a man, too. Mine left me for Paris."

"Do you have a penis?" Probably not the most appropriate question to be asking, but I doubted Mr. Dancy would fire me. Or with my luck, maybe he would.

Carlos flushed. "Yes, but what—"

"Then get lost. No penises allowed."

He went back to his table, staring at me like I'd lost my mind, and maybe I had. But I was allowed to brood, even for just today.

"Can I get your phone numbers?" I pulled out my new cell phone. I'd never owned one before and was still trying to figure out how to use it. "I don't have many friends left. Most are either dead or moved to Florida and Arizona. It'd be nice to have some girls to get together with."

"Sure." Piper reached for my phone and quickly added herself to my contacts, then handed it to Kerrie, who seemed to hesitate, but with a nod from Piper, she did the same.

"I was thinking," I said, chewing my bottom lip. "If you two aren't busy tonight, maybe we can have a boyfriend bonfire."

Kerrie's mouth dropped open a second time as she glanced at Piper. They both probably thought I was loony.

"I'm pretty sure burning exes is illegal." Piper laughed.

I laughed, too. "Well, I didn't mean burn our exes. I thought perhaps we needed a sort of cleansing ceremony. We could each bring something that our ex gave us to burn, kind of a good riddance to them type thing."

Piper shrugged. "I'm game. What time do you want us there and what's your address?"

"Does six sound good?" It'd been a while since I'd had company over, but it'd be nice to fill the house with some noise. Maybe it'd make me a little less lonely tonight.

"That'll work for me. Sophie will be home to watch the younger two," Kerrie said. "Now, I just have to decide what to bring."

I texted the girls my address, then finished eating my food before I had to go back to work. On my way home tonight, I'd have to stop to buy some lighter fluid. We already had a small stack of wood in the backyard, as well as a fire pit.

Maybe this would be good for me. Lord knows, things couldn't get any worse. Although, by saying that, I'd probably jinxed myself.

Chapter Ten

PIPER

"So, do you think it's odd that Maude all of a sudden invited us over?" I asked Kerrie, who was driving.

She flashed me a quick smile. "A little, but I guess not really. She knows we've both been through bad breakups and probably figured we'd be the best company. At least we can all commiserate with one another."

"You're right. I don't know what I'd do without you guys. But this has me kind of panicked. If Maude and Cornelius couldn't even stay together after that long, what hope do we have? Is there a point in me even dating Wooyoung?" I played with the frayed strings on my ripped jeans.

Kerrie peered at me when we came to a stop sign. "Yes. You need to at least try. If it doesn't work, then it doesn't work. Besides, he seems way too nice to play the same cheating ass game that Minho did."

I shrugged. "Maybe. Ugh! I guess you're right. I need to not freak out about this. Wooyoung and I are supposed to have dinner later when we're done exterminating our exes. So, I definitely don't want to psych myself out."

She laughed. "Christ, you make us sound like the Ghostbusters or something taking care of supernatural creatures."

"Well, that part *is* kind of true."

My phone alerted us to turn right. I hadn't realized Maude lived in this part of the suburbs of Chicago. There were a lot of older, more established houses and neighborhoods. They were a little more spread apart here than I'd thought they'd be. People had actual yards.

We pulled in front of a two-story white house with black shutters. A picket fence surrounded both the front yard and back, the house itself nestled safely behind the gate. She even had a couple of mature trees, which must've been there since before the house had been built.

A porch swing shifted in the breeze, the red checkered decorative pillows inviting us to take a seat and relax.

"This is a cute place," I said as we parked in the driveway behind Maude's car. I wasn't sure what I'd expected, but it wasn't this.

We climbed from the vehicle, both carrying a grocery bag with our chosen burn items. Maude met us on the porch wearing a bright pink tracksuit.

"Good, you guys found the house. I already have the wood in the fire pit." She smiled, ushering us inside.

"Do you need a permit to burn stuff?" I asked.

She waved me off. "Never have asked."

Kerrie quirked an eyebrow, her lips twitching as if trying not to smile.

"This is a beautiful house," Kerrie said, her gaze shifting around the room.

I took in the hardwood floors and glass roosters sitting atop the cupboards. The red and white checkerboard backsplash matched the pillows on the porch. It was very country-farm-chic.

"Thanks. Been here a long time. If you want to follow me, we can go into the backyard."

She led us down a hallway, past a laundry room and a bedroom, to a backdoor, which led to the yard. There were three camp chairs set up around the pit. At the back of the fence, there were two large maple trees, which I was sure were gorgeous in the autumn when the leaves changed colors.

"I made some lemonade and cookies if you girls want a snack." Maude pointed at a small picnic table under a plaid awning that came off the back of the house.

"Thanks, I might snag something. I haven't eaten dinner yet." I grabbed a chocolate chip cookie. "Oh, my God! This is so good. Are these homemade?"

"Yeah, I do a lot of baking from scratch." Maude smiled. "So, what did you girls bring to burn?" She reached for a bottle of lighter fluid and a long lighter that looked like a gun.

From her bag, Kerrie pulled out a pair of dark blue silk boxers. "These are Hal's favorite underwear, which are name brand and cost a fortune. And I'll throw these in for the fun of it." She held up a pack of condoms. "Found them in his wallet when I was grabbing Sophie some gas money to give her friend."

I snickered. "Well, he'll be surprised if he goes to get it on and has no protection."

"Yep."

Maude lit the fire and laughed. "Ah, that's genius. Are you sure you don't want to sell those underpants? Might be able to make a few bucks off 'em."

I sat down in one of the camp chairs. "Shit. That'd be funny. Put them up on eBay, maybe share the link with everyone on your social media."

She wrinkled her nose. "Just my luck, the kids would see it and click on it. Speaking of kids, I didn't tell you two about my latest mishap when I took Sophie driving the other night. A mishap my daughter has aptly named Dildo-Divorce-Gate."

"Do I even want to know about this?" I asked.

"Probably not, but you guys are going to hear all about it."

Kerrie told us about the runaway vibrator that'd fallen out of her glove box, and how the cop was her daughter's friend's dad.

"Why in God's name did you have a sex toy in your glove box?" Maude stopped stirring the now roaring fire and glanced between us.

"That is another embarrassing story involving my youngest daughter getting into my purse." Kerrie flushed scarlet as she explained the show-and-tell debacle.

"Sweet Mary, Mother of God. Remind me not to ride in your van with you. That sex toy is cursed."

I laughed. "It's something, but I think I'd get it out of your vehicle at this point."

"Agreed, I need to find a much better hiding spot."

"What did you bring, Piper?" Maude picked up a small box from one of the chairs.

"I brought a couple of things as well. I couldn't decide on just one. I brought the pillow Minho made me when we were in high school, which has our prom picture on it. I never want this thing near my head again." I tossed it onto the ground, then grabbed the decorative wooden box that had, at one time, held my engagement ring. I'd kept the box because it'd been so pretty. The ring I'd pawned soon after our split.

"Oh, I kind of like the box," Maude said. "But, if it's from your ex, it must go."

"And what about you?" I watched her grab a cardboard box.

"I've got Corny's old dentures. He won't be using these again anytime soon."

With a giggle, I said, "Wait, will those even burn?"

"We're about to find out. If not, I guess I'll have some creepy looking teeth at the bottom of my pit."

"Just your luck, the neighbors will think you murdered someone," Kerrie said.

"I'm sure they already believe that. Gotta keep 'em scared so they don't bug me." Maude cleared her throat, using her free hand to wave at the smoke in the air. "Okay, so let this bonfire be cleansing. Let us get rid of all the bad juju hanging around us. Today, we begin anew. No more letting these bastards ruin our lives. Try and see this as our closure."

"Hear, hear." Kerrie held up the boxers in a mock-cheer.

"Hear, hear," I repeated.

One by one, we tossed our items into the flickering flames. The pillow seemed to melt before my eyes, Minho's face disappearing one tiny detail at a time, which was sorta therapeutic.

We watched the fire for long minutes, none of us saying anything. It seemed so final. Like we were really closing this chapter of our lives. Although, I doubted it'd be that easy. However, it felt good to do it.

"To friendship," I said, moving to get a lemonade.

"To friendship," they both answered in response.

We toasted our boyfriend bonfire. A sense of belonging and peace fell over me for the first time in a long while.

"Oh, crap, I hate to break up our party, but I'm supposed to have dinner with Wooyoung." I set my cup back down.

"Of course. Thank you for stopping by. Maybe we can all get together again soon. Next time, for dinner or drinks or something of that sort."

"I'd like that." Kerrie nodded. "Lord knows, I don't hardly leave the house. School's almost done, so the kids will be on summer break. I'll be a little more available then."

"See you tomorrow at work, Maude." I waved as Kerrie and I headed out.

"Do you smell wood smoke?" Wooyoung asked as we made our way to the restaurant.

"Oh, shoot. That's me. I had a bonfire with Maude and Kerrie. Long story." I laughed when his eyebrows shot up.

"I see. Speaking of Maude, she was in a mood at work today. I've never heard her get that snappy with people before."

"Yeah, well, you'd be pissed too if your spouse of fifty years left you."

"You're lying," he said, mouth gaping like a bass trying to snag a worm.

"No. I'm so not. I feel really bad for her. None of us saw it coming, least of all her. I mean, two weeks ago, he was having lunch with her at work, everything seemed fine, and just like that, gone."

He frowned. "Maybe I'll try to do something nice for her. Grab her a coffee or donut on my way into work tomorrow."

"Speaking of grabbing stuff, I feel horrible you keep paying for all my coffee."

"Are you still going on about that?" he teased, reaching across to give my hand a squeeze. "Seriously, I don't mind. If I did, I wouldn't do it anymore."

"How is it you're so nice?"

He gave me a quick glance. "I'm not always nice. Ask my sister."

"Being mean to siblings doesn't count," I said. "Although, as an only child, I guess I'm not the best judge."

"So, your mom never had any more kids?" Wooyoung asked.

"God, no. She's been married like six or seven times—I lost count. But no, she only wanted to get fat once."

"Wait, your mom actually told you that?"

I laughed. "Yeah. That, and she doesn't have a great track record staying with any one man for very long. In my father's defense, he died. However, every other man she's divorced."

"I can't even imagine growing up in that kind of environment. My parents have been married for thirty-five years." He parked the car at the steakhouse, then shut off the engine.

"It kind of sucked. Although, I do love my stepdad, David. He was married to my mom for over five years. He's my favorite. He never had any other kids, so I'm pretty much his. I talk more to him than I do Mom. They got divorced right before my freshman year of high school."

"No wonder you have so many trust issues when it comes to relationships. First, your serial-marrying mother, and then Minho."

"True." I smiled at him before we climbed from the vehicle. "So, be gentle with me, Wooyoung."

He met me at the sidewalk and took my hand in his. The scent of grilled beef wafted in the air as someone came out of the restaurant. My stomach growled. Damn. It smelled so good. I couldn't wait to eat.

As soon as we stepped inside, we stood in line, waiting for the hostess.

"We should go somewhere else to eat?" Wooyoung's grip on my hand tightened.

"Why? What's wrong?" My eyes met his.

"Your ex is here." He nodded to a table near the door.

Sure enough. He was sitting in a booth, Hani right beside him, and an older couple whose faces I couldn't see seated across from them. I stiffened, shifting to stand behind Wooyoung.

"Okay. Yeah, let's find someplace else," I said as he led me back outside.

"If you want, we could grab takeout and go back to my place," he suggested.

"Are you sure?"

"Absolutely."

Before we drove off, Wooyoung called in an order. By the time we got to the Chinese Den, they had our food ready to go. A few minutes later, we parked in a garage under his apartment building, which wasn't too far from mine. It was fancier by far, but without my lake view.

We made our way into the lobby where he punched in a security code to get into the elevator. He hit the seventh floor button, and up we went. The elevator started to smell like my chicken fried rice and cheese wontons.

"I'm not sure I'll make it to your apartment before scarfing my food down."

He chuckled. "Well, we could just sit on the floor in here and eat, but I think the other residents might frown on that."

"Maybe. Or they'll think we're super creative with our picnic choice."

"Did you say picnic?" His eyes glittered. Their warm chocolate color nearly melted me, and my face heated. Phew, this boy could definitely turn on the charm.

"Yes."

"Hmm...I can arrange that. When we get inside, you stay in the entryway while I set things up."

"You really don't have to do that."

"No, but I want to."

When we got to his apartment, true to his word, he had me stand in the foyer. A few minutes later, he hollered, "Okay, you can come in now."

As I rounded the corner of the hallway, it opened into a living room with dark hardwood floors. Windows covered the whole back wall, giving an awesome view of the cityscape, which I was sure the loft above probably had an even better visual. He had brown leather furniture with lime, teal, and coral throw pillows, while another wall had a modern marble gas fireplace. Above that hung a flat screen TV. There were paintings of sunsets and beaches. The open room concept led right into the kitchen, which had all stainless-steel appliances and white granite countertops.

My eyes darted back to the checkered picnic tablecloth Wooyoung had spread out on the floor between the couch and recliner. The food was placed on fancy plates.

"This is perfect," I said.

He sat down, then patted the spot next to him. "Come, let's feed you, my hungry girl."

My hungry girl? I kind of liked the sound of that. It'd been so long since I felt like I belonged with someone.

I kicked off my shoes and plopped beside him. "You don't have to tell me twice."

We were silent while we ate, the only noise coming in the form of some light music he'd put on. It was kind of nice to know he seemed just as passionate about eating as I was. Minho normally picked his way around his plate. Although, maybe I shouldn't be comparing the two. When we finished dinner, I helped him gather our dishes and food items.

"Do you want to see the rest of the place?"

"Sure."

He guided me into a small bathroom off the living room, which was done in more of the same bright lime, teal, and coral colors. From there, he took me to the guest bedroom, then finally up a pair of metal industrial type stairs into a loft.

"Wow. This is perfect." I spun around. At the center of the room, there was a king-sized bed, covered in a teal comforter. From the bed, you could see through the windows below.

"I have two walk-in closets, and the master bathroom is pretty spectacular."

I slid into a large, tiled bathroom. The tub had jets in it, and there was a huge shower with room for more than one person. "Geez, how many people can you fit in your shower?"

"At least two." His voice had deepened, his face turning pink.

I swallowed hard, thinking how much I'd love to step into the shower. My gaze followed the line of his broad shoulders, down his narrow waist to his muscled thighs. Oh God. I needed to turn off my thoughts now. Butterflies flittered in my stomach.

"Um, that's the end of the tour, I guess," he said.

"I love your place. The view is amazing." I tried not to look at the shower again, but instead found myself lost in his gaze.

He took a step closer to me, his hand cupping my face. His lips pressed against mine, the faint remnant of lemonade left on his tongue as it danced against mine.

A soft moan escaped me as I wrapped my arms around his neck, tugging him closer. My body pressed against his so that I could feel the contours of his muscles as we embraced. His thumb traced my jawline, his mouth following a similar trail.

"Wooyoung," I whispered as he pulled back.

"I like you a lot, Piper, but we can take this as slow or as fast as you want."

"Okay." My fingers found the hair at the nape of his neck and tangled there, drawing his mouth down once more. This time, I kissed him. Heat radiated as he stroked my back, wedging me even closer. Even now, I felt the hardness between his legs.

But was I ready for this step? What if he hurt me? Damn, I wish my mind would just shut up. Let me bask in this moment.

I took a step away, my body on fire. "I...I like you, too, Wooyoung. But I think I'll need to take things slow."

"Alright." He smiled, brushing strands of hair from my face. "However you want to do this is fine with me. I'm not going any-where."

I hugged him, loving the feel of his arms around me. "Thank you."

"You don't have to thank me, Piper."

Maybe not, but I appreciated the fact he was willing to take this at my pace.

Chapter Eleven

KERRIE

"Hal, where are you?" I practically yelled into the phone receiver. "Sophie and I need to leave for the concert. You said you'd be able to watch the younger two tonight."

Christ. I should've made other arrangements. He never followed through with anything.

Sophie stared at me, her eyes darting to the clock again. We still had plenty of time, but we needed to get checked into the hotel, then walk over to the United Center.

"That's tonight? Crap, I forgot." I heard the clink of silverware hitting a plate. "I stopped to get dinner."

An exasperated sigh escaped my lips. "Well, if you'd like, I can call your parents and ask if I can drop the kids off with them."

"No. I…I'll get home. I'm getting the bill now. I'll be there in fifteen," he said.

Was he afraid I would blurt out details of our divorce to his parents?

"Mom?" Sophie said.

"He's on his way. Fifteen minutes, tops. If he's not here by then, I'll get ahold of Grandma and Grandpa."

"I swear, he's such a jerk. He's probably eating dinner with his new girlfriend."

"Who's got a new girlfriend?" Tommy asked, hopping over to us with his hat pulled down over his eyes. He nearly collided with the kitchen counter.

"Hey, let's take the hat off before you get hurt. And no one has a girlfriend," I said.

Sophie shrugged, then took a small mirror from her crossover purse. She reapplied lip gloss, smacking her lips together. She wore a black t-shirt with a large green seven in the middle, which according to her was part of the band's logo. It was a K-pop group she'd come across two years ago, and had since become obsessed with. Not that I blamed her. The music was pretty good, and the band members were admittedly adorable.

I'd spent the last week watching videos of them with Sophie to prepare for the concert. I even learned their fan-chant. The things I did for my kids, I tell you.

"I can't believe we're actually going." Sophie smiled. "I'm going to take so many pictures and videos. Oh, and Mya said they got the room next to ours, so maybe we can all hang out after the show."

"I doubt you're going to have a voice left after the concert." I laughed.

"Does my makeup look okay?" She peered over at me, her dark hair hung straight to the middle of her back, her brown eyes sparkling and big beneath the glittering green shades of eye shadow she used to coordinate with the group's color.

"Yes, it looks perfect!"

Soon, Hal came barging into the house. "I'm home. Sorry about that."

"Since you forgot it was my birthday, can you at least give me some spending money to get a t-shirt while I'm at the show?' Sophie held out her hand, eyes narrowed.

Dang. I needed to take a page out of the Sophie Holloway book of nasty expressions. The girl had it down pat. Too bad I wasn't more assertive like her, then maybe I wouldn't be in this predicament.

"Sure. Be good and have fun tonight." He reached into his back pocket and pulled out some cash. He then gave her a quick hug.

"Daddy, you're home tonight." Tommy latched onto his leg. "Let's play Legos."

"Yeah, let's play Legos." Nella joined him, clinging to his other leg.

I smiled. Finally, he could play Dad for one night. He'd be the one to stop all the fights, figure out food, and make sure they got to bed.

"Be good, guys, see you tomorrow."

Sophie and I hurried out the door, our overnight bags already loaded into the van. It took us a while to get across town. The traffic closer to the arena was already backed up, even though the show didn't start for a couple of hours yet.

I found a spot to park in the hotel lot, then we went inside to get our room situated.

"Mya said they're already here." Sophie peered at her phone. "They're in room 127. I wonder if the adjoining door between our rooms opens."

I snickered. "I guess we'll find out."

It'd been a long time since I'd stayed in a hotel. It'd be nice to be able to sleep in and to have breakfast prepared for me. And for once, someone else could fold the towels and make the bed.

When we got to the room, I immediately dropped my bag on the floor and threw myself back on one of the two queen beds, which were covered in matching blue, red, and gold comforters. A large screen TV hung on the wall while a small couch sat in front of the window overlooking the city. I hopped up and went to check out the large bathroom.

"I love this tub and shower. It has jets on the tub." Maybe after a long night of standing up and screaming, I could come back and bask in the Jacuzzi. Order some wine from room service... That'd be the life.

A knock sounded on the door, and then squeeing commenced.

I came out to find Mya hugging Sophie. Mya's brown skin glistened with the same green glitter eyeshadow my daughter's did. Her long braids were pulled back with green ribbon.

"Okay, so I know you said no birthday present, but I couldn't resist." Mya held up a box for her.

"What is it?"

"Open it and find out." She held her hands together in anticipation as she waited for Sophie.

"Oh. My. God. You got me a light stick! I love you." Sophie pulled out a flashlight looking thing with the shape of a bird on top of it. When she turned it on, the light glowed green.

"So, I guess the light sticks are popular with K-pop groups," a new voice said from behind Mya.

I glanced up to see the very same police officer who'd pulled us over during Dildo-Divorce-Gate. "Um, Mr. ...Officer Walker. I...well, hi," I stammered. Dear God. Why? Maybe he'd forgotten about the incident.

He grinned. "Ms. Holloway, I thought we established last time we talked that I'm Demarcus."

"Yes, Demarcus. Right."

Holy hell. My cheeks flushed. Phew, if I thought he looked good in his uniform, he looked even hotter in his tight black shirt, which showed some massive guns, if I do say so myself. And I don't mean the carrying kind. His jeans sat snug against his waist, his muscular thighs evident beneath the fabric.

I swallowed hard. Biting my lip, I quickly brought my gaze back to his face where I found his beautiful smile waiting for me. Seeing him here like this made me all too aware I hadn't been touched by a man in a long time. Wow, it'd taken like two seconds for my mind to jump down that rabbit hole.

"And I'm Kerrie, not Ms. Holloway."

"I'll remember that. Sorry if I startled you. Mya's mom, my ex, Cheyenne, was supposed to come with her, but our son Mackai got sick. He only wants his mom when he doesn't feel good. So, we decided to switch duties tonight. I'm on concert watch with Mya, and she's taking care of Mackai."

"I hope he feels better."

"Just a flu bug. So, what exactly do you think we've gotten ourselves into?" He turned to take in the scene of our girls freaking out.

"I have no idea, but I think it'll involve lots of screaming, swooning, and possibly some ear damage." I laughed.

He held up a pair of earplugs. "I'll at least try to save my ears. I have an extra pair if you find yourself in need of them."

Smiling, I nodded. "And I might take you up on that. So, did you also learn the fan chant for tonight?"

He sighed. "Do I get extra cool dad points if I say yes?"

"Of course."

"Mom, Mya said they're selling t-shirts outside the venue right now. Can we go and try to get one before the concert starts?"

"Sure. Let me grab my wallet," I said, hurrying to find my purse.

"Dad gave me money. I should be fine."

"I know, but you might get thirsty or hungry or something." I'd set aside a small amount to spend for tonight. "Besides, it's your seventeenth birthday, it's supposed to be special."

"It already is. The fact that we're here."

"Dad, can we go down with them? I want to see what other kind of merch they have." Mya looped her arm through Sophie's.

"Yeah, might as well. We can get in line for the concert when you two are done."

We traipsed after the girls. Demarcus's hand brushed against mine and my pulse nearly exploded my veins like a grenade.

"Sorry," I said, shifting a step away.

"No problem. It's hard not to bump into each other with the amount of people out here tonight." He glanced around, side-stepping a teen girl who was running to her friends. "Have you stayed away from trouble since last I saw you? No more traffic stops?"

I nearly choked on the piece of gum I was chewing. "Um, yeah, no more trouble. Also, that is hands-down the most embarrassing thing that's ever happened to me."

He chuckled, peering at me. "Like I said before, I've seen much worse things fall out of glove box."

Of course, I couldn't get lucky and have him forget. I rubbed a hand across my burning cheeks. "Yeah, like what?"

"One time, I pulled over a serial killer. Only at the time, I didn't know he was. At least, not until a severed hand toppled from beneath his registration and insurance papers."

"You're kidding?" My nose wrinkled.

"I wish I was. Another time, we had to search a kid's car, and he had a bunch of used condoms stashed in there so his mom wouldn't know he was having sex. So, that was another fun one."

This time, I giggled. "Alright, so I'm definitely not the worst one. But for me, knowing you're Mya's dad made it worse. Because there's the potential of bumping into you since our daughters are friends."

"And I'll probably never let you live it down." His grin widened. Was there no end to his perfect smiles?

We waited in line for t-shirts for forty-five minutes, then, once the girls had what they wanted, we headed to the venue, where we had another thirty-minute wait in the late afternoon heat.

"I'm thinking I should've brought an umbrella to shield me from the sun." I wiped the sweat beading on my brow.

"No joke." He dabbed at his own forehead. "The things we do for our kids. Speaking of kids, Mya mentioned you and your husband got divorced."

Ah hell, Demarcus sure had a way of getting straight to the point. Hopefully, this didn't get out to too many people or Hal would be ticked. "Yes. We did, earlier this year. I still live at the house with him until I can save up to move out on my own. Which, I know sounds strange, but Hal's on the road a lot so I don't see him a ton." Other than when he was sneaking scantily clad women into our house, whom my children mistook for peeping toms.

"So, you guys get along?"

"Eh, depends on the day." I laughed. "He's kind of a pain when it comes to actually parenting."

"Sophie let on about that. Sorry if it seems like I'm prying." His brow furrowed.

"No, it's fine. Very few people actually know we're divorced. It's nice to be able to talk about it."

"If you ever need anything, and he's not around, give me a call. I'm pretty handy around the house or if you need someone to talk to. I have the kids, week on, week off, so there are times when I'm not working that it can get too quiet." He took out his cell. "Do you have your phone on you? We can exchange numbers now if you'd like."

"Of course." I reached into my back pocket and slid my phone from my jeans. I brought up my contact page and handed it to him, and he did the same, handing me his phone. Once I typed in my info, I gave it back to him, noticing his screensaver was a picture of him with his kids. They all looked so happy. I wondered if he had a girlfriend. Not that dating ranked high on my priority list at this point.

"There, now you can get a hold of me anytime you want."

"Thanks, I appreciate it. Are you and your ex on good terms?"

"Mostly. We want to co-parent our kids and make sure they know we both love them. We try not to step on one another's toes. I think we get along better now than we ever did when we were married. After we had our youngest, we realized we were in very different places. She's an architect and would have meetings all the time with clients, while I was working all kinds of crazy hours doing patrols. We talk at least every other day to keep one another up to date on the kids' activities."

"I wish Hal was like that. Sometimes, I wonder if he remembers we have kids." A sharp edge entered my voice.

"It's his loss, and one day, he's going to look back and realize how stupid he was."

I hoped Demarcus was right, and I also hoped that time would come sooner rather than later.

The line started moving and we entered the venue. We found our seats about ten rows up from the floor, giving us a great view of the center stage.

"Mom, can you swap seats so Mya and I can sit next to one another?" Sophie asked.

"Sure."

Mya climbed around my legs, and I slid in next to Demarcus.

"I guess you and I are on our own now."

We glanced at the girls who were already snapping pictures of the stage and each other.

"Dad, move closer to Kerrie so I can get your pics." Mya held up her phone in our direction.

"Oh, I want one, too. Don't move," Sophie said, grabbing her cell.

Demarcus and I leaned in. He bent down so his face was level with mine, his cologne nearly undoing me. He not only looked good, but the man smelled damn good, too. His hand rested lightly on my shoulder, and I swallowed hard.

Just when they finished with the picture taking, the arena went dark and low music started. Screaming erupted all round us as glow sticks turned on. The heavy thump of a bass drum made me jump as, one by one, green laser lights turned on around the stage.

For almost two hours, music and screams pounded. Fans did different chants along with the songs. Sophie seemed so happy. The smile never leaving her face until a sad song came on. Seeing her like this made me happy, too. She deserved tonight. To let loose. To be normal and not have to worry about me and Hal. And for the first time in a long time, I felt at ease also.

When the concert ended, we poured onto the street with the steady stream of people and headed to the hotel.

"Oh, my gosh, did you see Youngjae's dance at the end? Holy hotness." Sophie gripped tight to Mya's arm.

"Girl, all I saw were Jackson's abs. That boy is ripped."

"I think this is where I put my earplugs back in," Demarcus said beside me.

"Aw, c'mon, you're no fun." I dropped my voice to a whisper. "Be glad this is all they're talking about."

He quirked an eyebrow. "The first thing I do when she brings up a boy is take out my badge and ask where he lives."

"No, you don't!"

"I do."

"Damn. Count me glad you weren't my dad growing up."

"I'm glad, too." His gaze met mine.

Was he flirting? My teeth grazed my bottom lip, legs trembling beneath me. Damn, this man was giving me fanny flutters.

When we got back inside and up to our hall, Sophie turned to me.

"Mom, can Mya come hang with me in our room for a while?"

"Sure, are you okay with that?" I asked Demarcus.

"Yeah. Tell you what, Kerrie, if you want to come watch TV in our room, we can let the girls have some time to themselves."

"Sure, just let me drop my wallet off." Phew, I had no idea what to think. "Make sure you girls stay in the room, okay?"

"We will, Mom." Sophie turned to whisper something to Mya, and they giggled.

I had no idea what they were up to, but hopefully they listened and stayed put. Shutting the door behind me, I did a quick breath check in my hand before knocking on Demarcus's room. He answered and ushered me inside.

"There isn't much on TV, but I figured we could give the girls a chance to do their thing. Maybe they'll get all the guy talk and giggling out of their system before we go to bed."

I followed him over to the couch, where I found a late-night talk show on. I plopped down, and he sat beside me.

We were quiet for a second, until he turned to me.

"I don't want to come on strong or anything, but I had fun tonight and wondered if you might be interested in going out sometime?"

I wet my lips, hearting thudding like a car on a speedbump. "I had fun tonight, too, and I'd love to get together."

"The girls will be thrilled to hear that," he said.

"Wait, did they know you were going to ask me out?" My eyes widened.

"No, but I overheard them talking about how good we got along, then Mya said something like 'maybe they'll date.' So, I couldn't disappointment them."

I laughed. "Hopefully that's not the only reason you're asking me out."

"It's not. I promise. You're very beautiful, funny, and kind. And I can tell you're a good mom. Sophie talks about you a lot when she's over."

"And here I thought I was the uncool, mean Mom," I said.

"I assure you, you're not."

Our gazes met, his coffee-colored eyes nearly burning me on the spot. His fingers swiped a stray curl from my cheek, and leaned in. A moment later, his lips met mine. Heat raced through me like molten lava flowing from a volcano. Slow, steady, and incinerating everything in contact.

My mouth moved against his, the taste of spearmint fresh on his breath. A soft moan escaped my lips as my fingers slid up his muscled chest and circled his neck.

Oh God. His kisses were amazing. And all I could think was I wanted more.

Then, I remembered my Spanx, and my stretch marks covering belly. I definitely wasn't young anymore. Would he still be attracted to me if he saw what was underneath the clothes? Hal certainly didn't think I was perky anymore.

But the worries quickly drifted away as we reclined on the couch, until he laid on top of me. Through our clothing, I felt his desire for me. He eased away from my lips, trailing stray kisses down my neck while his hand cupped my breast.

At least I'd remembered to wear my nice black lace bra. One of only a few pieces of sexy clothing I owned. I made a mental note to take a trip to the mall to update my lingerie. Not that I expected to be taking my clothes off a lot. I just wanted to look okay if I did.

Giggling came from outside our door, then the beep from the room key unlocking the door.

We leapt a part, and Demarcus quickly sat up, grabbing one of the throw pillows and set it in his lap while I adjusted my shirt and hair. I didn't need a mirror to know I was blushing.

"Why do I feel like my parents just walked in on me having sex?" Demarcus whispered.

I smirked. "It kind of does, only is it worse if it's our kids?"

"One hundred percent, yes." He chuckled.

The girls came in carrying junk food.

"We brought snacks," Sophie said.

"Good, I'm hungry." Demarcus caught my eye. And I couldn't help but wonder if he meant what I thought he did.

He and I weren't left alone for the rest of the night, which I wasn't sure if I was grateful for or bummed. It'd been a long time since I'd been with anyone.

When Sophie and I finally got back to our room, it was two in the morning. I changed into my pajamas, and before I flipped off my light, I noticed I had a text from Demarcus.

Demarcus: *I was serious about what I said. I want to see you again. Maybe dinner soon?*

Me: *I'd love that. Sweet dreams, and thank you for a great night.*

Demarcus: *Sweet dreams to you, too. See you tomorrow.*

I hoped so. I didn't want to get my hopes up. After all, Hal said I was boring. What if Demarcus thought so, too?

Chapter Twelve
MAUDE

My wrinkled hand traced the rim of my coffee mug as Mr. Dancy came into the conference room, his dress shirt sleeves pushed up to his elbows. Already, there were beads of sweat on his forehead. Good God. If he'd just turn up the air, but he'd rather us all suffer. I'd taken my purple jacket off the moment I'd walked into the building.

"Good, you're all here. It's been a couple of weeks since we had a sit-down meeting together."

Piper peered at me and rolled her eyes. I raised my cup to her.

Mr. Dancy seemed flustered as he sat at the head of the table like our patriarch was ready to ground us all for misbehavior or whatnot.

"I've called this meeting as I feel that everyone is not taking our greeting cards seriously. There's far too much cynicism as of late. All of you here used to know how to write beautiful lines about love and caring and being together. Now, I feel as if I'm the ringmaster of a circus." He gave a dramatic pause, turning his gaze on Piper, Kerrie, and Carlos. "And you three have rubbed off on Maude. The one person I could always count on."

I snorted. "They didn't rub off on me. I came to my own conclusions about the opposite sex and this notion of true love."

Mr. Dancy waved his hand like he was swatting away a fly. "Eh, we're not going to argue or carry on about this. I simply brought it up because I've come up with a plan."

Oh, boy, here we go.

"We're going to go on a work retreat to help fix things. I understand that sometimes life throws us limes."

"You mean lemons?" I asked.

"No—limes. You have your sayings, I have mine, and mine include limes. Now, if you'll let me finish." His brow furrowed while he tapped his fingers against the table in what I assumed was annoyance. "I want you to set aside the last weekend in June for a work retreat."

"What?" Kerrie glanced at the rest of us.

What was right. In all the years I'd been here, that man had never splurged on anything for us. No gifts at Christmas, no extra time off. No jelly of the month club. Nope, no frills from him.

"A retreat," Mr. Dancy repeated. "You'll all be pampered. Consider it a spa type weekend, filled with team building and rejuvenating."

"You're serious?" Piper said, leaning back in her chair as if in disbelief.

"Very. That's what this meeting was called for. Just wanted to give you a heads up, so you can make arrangements on your calendars for that weekend. I'll give you further details by Friday. Now, everyone back to work."

He slid from the conference room as quickly as he'd come in.

"What's come over him?" I spun my chair to face Piper and Kerrie. "Mr. Cheap Pants can't even be persuaded to spring for a constant flow of air conditioning, let alone a spa day."

"Hmm...I'm feeling very suspicious," Piper said. "Maybe he's planning on closing down the business and wants to do one last thing for us?" She chewed the end of her pen.

"No, I think it's a ploy to make us work a weekend," Kerrie said.

"Wouldn't that be a kicker? Ah well, at least we'll get to do it some place nice. I wonder if we can get one of those massages. The ones where they make you lay on a table. I always see them in movies and think I'd like to try one. Although, I doubt anyone wants to see my wrinkled-up lady parts." I chuckled to myself.

"They cover you up with sheets or towels," Piper said. "So, no one but the masseuse would see you."

"Oh, you've had one before?"

"Yeah, my mom paid for one after forgetting to call me on Christmas when she was in Italy two years ago."

"Like I said, workday or not, at least we'll get something out of it. Hope it's a beach front spa."

"Speaking of workday, I suppose we should probably start ours. I doubt Mr. Dancy's generous attitude will last too much longer if we don't get busy." Kerrie grabbed her notepad, pen, and cup.

We stood, making our way to our offices. I watched as Wooyoung hung back to walk with Piper. They seemed awfully cozy with one another since I'd come back to work. I hoped he didn't turn into a

Minho or Corny. My eyes narrowed at the back of his head, willing him to not screw this up.

"You're glaring," Kerrie said from beside me.

"I suppose I am. Been doing a lot of that lately. How are things with your kids? Any more toy mishaps?"

She flushed. "Luckily, no. Back to our normal routine of homework, running, and all out chaos. I'm so glad the school year is almost done. At least then, I won't have to worry about commuting them every morning."

I gave a sad smile, thinking of my late son. "One day, you'll miss all that."

We parted ways when we reached our offices, and I went in and pulled up a few ideas I'd been working on prior to Corny leaving. So far, nothing came to me. I now understood the rut Piper had. It's hard to write about true love when someone completely destroys you and everything that forever even stood for.

I sat staring at my screen for hours until I heard my coworkers going to lunch. With a sigh, I locked my computer, and went to grab my food.

"What do you girls say we head over to the park and eat there today? It'd be a nice change from the cafeteria," I suggested.

Piper grinned. "Yes, I could use some fresh air, and maybe a breeze under the trees. I'm dying of heat exhaustion."

"I second that. I need to air out." Kerrie fanned her face with her hand.

We headed for the front door and moved down the sidewalk to a small park at the end of the block. It had some benches, a couple of picnic tables, and mature trees. I picked a table in the shade, and moved to sit down.

Piper and Kerrie sat across from me, spreading their food out in front of them.

"So, I never got the chance to tell you guys, but remember the cop from Dildo-Divorce-Gate?"

"Sophie's friend's dad, right?" Piper licked yogurt from her plastic spoon.

"Yes, Demarcus. He ended up going to the concert with us as Mya's mom had something come up, and well, we sorta made out in the hotel room after the concert."

"What? No way? Was he a good kisser?" Piper leaned closer, and I found myself doing the same.

"Oh. My. God. Yes. But then the girls came back and nearly caught us."

"Do you like him?" I asked, unwrapping a tuna salad sandwich.

Her cheeks reddened. "Of course, I mean we got a little hot and heavy."

I laughed. "Just because you fool around with someone, doesn't always mean you like 'em, so I had to ask."

"True, Maude has a point. Look at my mom, for hell's sake. She's been married six or seven times, and I can say I don't think it's because she loved every one of them."

"Hot damn! Your mom's been married that many times? And here I thought one man for fifty years was pretty spectacular. But that's like, what, a new man every three to five years?"

Piper groaned. "When you say it like that, it sounds even worse."

I finished my sandwich and carrot sticks, then stood to go throw away my trash. When I got near the tree, a squirrel climbed down next to me. "Hi there, fella, what are you doing?"

It bobbed its head, then in one swift motion, it ran up my pant leg.

I gasped, feeling the skittering of its nails on my skin as it moved closer to my thigh.

"Help! Oh, sweet Jesus, it's going to give me rabies." I shook my leg, horrified, trying not to topple over.

"Wait, hold still!" Piper screamed, hopping to come help me.

Kerrie followed, waving her arms for me to stop as she reached for my arm. "Piper's right, quit moving."

"I can't hold still! It might bite me."

Wooyoung bounded over out of nowhere like Superman in the guise of Clark Kent. "What's going on?"

I'd already reached for my button, ready to shed my work trousers. "A squirrel—"

"Hold still." He clutched my leg and tried reaching up my pants to get it. A second later, he caught the squirrel and pulled it out by the tail.

Thankfully, the small beast had only grabbed tight to the fabric of my pants and not the flesh on my leg. It instantly tore away from Wooyoung and rushed back up the tree.

"Well, I have to say, that's the most action I've had in a while." Heart beating frantically, I collapsed on the picnic table bench, panting. "I think I need to sit for a second, maybe grab a cigarette to smoke."

"You don't smoke." Kerrie quirked an eyebrow.

"I might have to start after this."

Trudging into the kitchen after work, I dropped my things on the counter along with the junk mail I'd grabbed from the box. My gaze flickered around the room to where Corny's old flannel jacket hung on a hook by the door. I still hadn't gathered the strength to get rid of it. Lying bastard or not, we'd been married a long time. My feelings weren't something I could just turn off, no matter how much I pretended.

My fingers gripped tight to the edge of the table as I steadied myself. Did this get any easier? Fighting back tears, I went over to his jacket and picked it up, holding it to my face. I inhaled deeply, catching the faint scent of his aftershave still clinging to the collar.

Why? Why did you have to leave me alone like this? We were supposed to be together forever. I wanted him here. To hold me. To let me yell at him, and to thump him in the ass for deserting me like this. My eyes watered and my throat closed.

Damn him.

I released the piece of clothing and headed into the living room just in time for a loud obnoxious knock on the front door. Muttering under my breath, I went to see who it was.

I found Griff, my next-door neighbor, standing on the porch with a bouquet of what looked like flowers picked from my own yard.

"Jesus H. Christ. My husband's only been gone for a few weeks."

"I know, Maude, but people our age have to strike while the iron's hot."

My lips pursed. "My iron won't ever be hot for you! Now, get out of here." I slammed the door shut.

"If you change your mind, I'll be at my house all night," he shouted from the other side of the wooden barrier.

Taking a deep breath, I peeled back the curtain to realize he'd dropped the flowers on the doorstep. The least he could've done was not leave them in a mess on my stoop. Jerk.

I needed a drink. A very strong drink. Without a second thought, I went to the kitchen to get my cell phone. Squinting, I scrolled my contacts until I found Piper's name.

I hit the green call button and waited for her to pick up.

"Hey, Piper. It's Maude. I know this is kind of last minute, but I wondered if you and Kerrie might want to go grab a drink and maybe dinner with me? I had a bad run-in with my overly sexual neighbor."

"Um, what do you mean, overly sexual?" she asked, her voice full of concern.

"I mean, the twit won't quit hitting on me. Ever since he found out Corny's gone, he's been showing up, throwing himself at me. The man is desperate. I don't think he's had anyone since old Betty down the road kicked the bucket a couple of years ago. And before Betty there was his wife, who left him for another woman about twenty years ago. Can definitely see why."

"Oh. Sure, I'll get ahold of Kerrie. Do you want us to pick you up? Or meet you somewhere?'

"Why don't you swing by and get me. I'll change really quick and be waiting on the porch."

About twenty-five minutes later, the girls pulled up in Kerrie's minivan. Both had traded their work clothes for jeans and nice tops, and of course, perfect makeup.

Oh, to be young again.

I glanced at my black slacks, red shirt, and matching red heels. Maybe I was overdressed for the bar, but I didn't own any jeans. If I asked, I bet Piper and Kerrie would shop with me sometime.

"Thank you for coming. It's been a crazy day," I said.

Kerrie glanced at the house next door. "Is that the guy who's bothering you?"

My eyes narrowed on the window where Griff had the curtain pulled back, staring. He gave a wave and big smile.

"Hellfire on Earth. Yes, that's the dope who won't leave me alone." I shook my fist at him, and he came out onto his porch, not the least bit concerned he was annoying me.

"Where you off to Maude?"

"None of your business, Griff. Have a good night."

"You left the flowers on your porch," he called after me.

"You mean the flowers you picked from my yard?"

"Hey, it's the thought that counts." He grinned, waggling his eyebrows.

"Cheapskate." I climbed into the van.

"Wow, that guy is something," Piper said. "He reminds me of one of those old crime bosses with his white tank top and over the top gold chain necklace."

"Tell me about it. You think he's bad, you should see his son, Sal. A hundred times worse."

"Was he friends with Cornelius?" Piper asked from the front seat.

"Unfortunately, yes. They got together all the time with the guys to play poker. A night I always made sure to not be around for."

"Wait, did he hit on you when your husband was around?" Kerrie caught my eye in the rearview mirror.

"He made sure Corny knew that if he ever screwed up, he'd swoop in."

"Swoop in like a vulture, you mean?" Piper laughed.

"He does sort of look like one of those carrion birds, doesn't he? Trying to peck around for leftovers."

"Where do you guys want to go?" Kerrie spun to face me from the driver's seat.

"How about Valentino's? They've got a great selection of drinks, and their burgers are pretty good, too." Corny and I would have a night out there about once a month. We'd watch whatever sport game was in season, and throw back a beer. No girly drinks for me. It was someplace comfortable and familiar.

When we got to the bar, we headed toward the back where it was darker and less crowded. Already, I smelled burgers cooking, and my stomach growled. It'd been a while since I'd been here. I swallowed hard, trying not to think about Corny. At least Piper and Kerrie chose a spot that was away from the table Corny and I used to always get.

We ordered drinks, or at least Kerrie and I did. Piper stuck with a diet pop and a burger.

"So, you and Wooyoung, huh?" I smiled.

"Yeah, who knew? He's super sweet, and gorgeous, but I'm also not getting my hopes up too high. We all know how quickly relationships can go to shit."

"That we do." I nodded. "To the girls." I raised my glass in a cheer.

"To the girls," they said in unison.

It felt nice to be out doing something and not sitting at home basking in the silence of the house—a place that held a memory in every corner. Somedays, I wanted to curl up in a ball and not leave the safe cocoon of my room. And other days, like today, it was too much to be there alone. I could see how someone could waste away.

We'd finished eating our food and ordered another round of drinks when I glanced up to find Griff walking into the bar with his friend, Tony, and his son, Sal.

Good grief. They looked like they were coming straight from the set of a seventy's mafia flick.

When Griff saw me, he smiled and headed toward us. "Maude, fancy meeting you here. It must be fate." He sidled up to me.

"You call it fate, I call it stalking. Now, go on, I'm having drinks with the girls."

"How about me and the boys join you?" He put his hand on my back.

I glowered. "Sweet Jesus, can't you take a hint? I'm not interested."

"Fine. How about I go and get a drink, then I'll come back to see if you changed your mind?"

"Or not. She said no." Piper set her fork down.

Man alive, her voice gave no room to argue, that was for sure. I was even more glad I'd invited Piper and Kerrie to come with me.

Griff snorted, then sauntered away like he owned the place. He sat at the bar, throwing back some shots. Not that I wanted to watch him, but he irritated me enough to make me want to keep an eye on him.

The girls and I discussed a possible shopping trip to help me update my wardrobe, both throwing out style ideas and showing me pictures on their phones. There were so many places online to order clothes nowadays, it was baffling.

About an hour later, Griff staggered back over to us. "Maude, why do you think you're too good for me?" He reached out to steady himself, but his hand clamped onto my breast. He chuckled to himself.

I let out a gasp, hopped to my feet, grabbed my purse, and then slapped him as hard as I could with it. "How dare you, you dirty bastard."

"Ow." He fell back into the table behind him, then launched himself upright.

"Don't hit my dad." Sal came closer, trying to grab hold of my arm, but Piper shot to her feet and knocked his hands away.

"Don't touch her. Tell your dad to leave her the hell alone. And no more copping cheap feels."

"Listen here, you mouthy bitch." He gave her a slight push.

Piper rushed at him, hand fisted, striking him in the face. She caught him in the nose, and it immediately started to bleed.

He staggered back, trying to regain his balance. His eyes darkened as he reached up to wipe his face. "What the fuck is wrong with you? You gave me a bloody nose."

Holy hell, I never knew she had that in her.

"Be glad that's all I gave you!" Piper shook her hand out.

Next thing I knew, Tony and Kerrie had joined in, and glasses and chairs were being thrown. Curse words were shouted. Complete chaos, was what it was. I crouched as a fork came bulleting at me. Hot damn, this was getting serious. It was like a warzone.

Tony gripped part of Kerrie's shirt as if to hold her in place. I took off my heel and wacked it across his arm.

"Let her go, you oaf!"

"Stop, or I'm calling the cops." The bartender barreled out from behind the counter.

But we didn't listen.

If Griff thought for one second he was going to get away with touching my breast, he had another think coming.

"Maude, look out," Piper cried.

A basket of peanuts came flying toward my face. This time, I ducked too late and ended up with salt in my eyes.

"Son of a—"

The door banged against the wall. Police burst in, bringing back memories of the last time I went to jail for marching with some civil rights activists. But this was far worse than that.

Glancing at the girls, I noted the shock on their faces as we were told to stop and put our hands up.

Chapter Thirteen

PIPER

My heart hammered in my chest as I attempted to raise my arms above my head. Oh God. I'd never had a run in with the police before. Not even a speeding ticket.

Sal, whose arms had only moments ago held me in a headlock, straightened suddenly with his hands up, crying like a baby.

"What is going on in here?" One of the officers trailed their gaze over us, gun drawn.

"Are you the only officer who works in Chicago?" Kerrie asked from beside me.

I followed her gaze to a tall man with dark skin and a gaze that burned like a hot cup of coffee.

He seemed startled. "Ker—I mean, Ms. Holloway? What are you doing here?"

"Um, trying to have a drink with my friends until that man," she nodded at Griff, but kept her hands over her head, "decided to grope our friend."

"I didn't grope her on purpose. I tripped and that's where my hand landed, her breast." He gave a shrug like it was no big deal. "The crazy woman came at me, striking me in the face with her luggage."

"It was my purse, you fool. And don't you tell me it was an accident. I saw you smile as soon as you did it." Maude snarled, nearly launching herself at him again. "You've been trying for years to seduce me, you dirty old man."

I reached out with one hand and caught her, keeping her in place, while I kept my other hand in the air. "Maude, now might not be the time for that."

"She's right. I need everyone to calm down so we can take statements."

"Can this be my statement?" Sal pointed to his bloody nose, where I'd landed a punch. "First, that old broad attacks my dad, and I try to come to his aid, then this twit punches me."

"You totally deserved it." My voice rose several octaves in defense, but I quickly shut my mouth to keep from incriminating myself further.

"This is what I get for picking up an extra shift tonight," the officer that seemed to know Kerrie said.

Then, it dawned on me. This must be Demarcus, the guy she'd made out with after the concert. Officer of the Dildo-Divorce-Gate as Kerrie had dubbed it.

"Please don't tell Sophie about this. I've never been in trouble before," Kerrie cried. Her brows furrowed, tears streaming down her face.

"I don't generally discuss work with my kids." His gaze softened momentarily, but then he went right back to work.

"I told them to knock it off," the bartender said loud enough for us all to hear. "I didn't want any trouble. But not a damn one of them listened. I can't run a bar with people fighting and scaring off all my customers."

My gaze narrowed. I had half a mind to design a 'shut the hell up' card line specifically for this guy. Not that we weren't in the wrong, but shit, he acted like we were hardened criminals and had set out to ruin the joint.

After the officers took all our statements, they came over. "We're going to have to bring you in," Officer Walker said.

Then they read us our rights.

I squeezed my eyes shut. Wonderful. I'd seen this procedure several times on TV, but I never thought I'd be the one getting arrested.

"Wait, what are our charges?" I asked, mouth dry like I'd sucked on a bag of cotton balls. Not that it mattered at this point what our charges were. The fact was, we were being hauled off to jail.

Officer Walker peered over at me. "Disorderly conduct."

I had no idea what that even meant. Was it a misdemeanor? A felony? How much time would I have to serve? Oh man, I didn't want to wear an orange jumpsuit and get beat up in the showers or be forced to become someone's lover. I'd seen this on TV, too.

Once we'd been patted down, Maude, Kerrie, and I were loaded into one patrol car while the guys were loaded into the other.

Kerrie sat between me and Maude, her mascara smeared on her cheeks. "He's never going to want to see me again after this. D-do you think they'll let us make a phone call? I need to let Sophie know I won't be home tonight. Jesus, this is such a mess."

"Shh, it'll be alright. We'll get it figured out."

"That damn Griff. This is all his fault," Maude snapped. "If it wasn't for his wanton needs and boob grabbing, we never would've had to fight."

It took us about twenty minutes to get to the jail, at which time we were brought through a heavy metal door and down a narrow hallway.

Already, the heat in the building overwhelmed me. The air was stale and smelled like various body odors. There were several cells we passed by, but they weren't like the ones in movies with the metal bars. These were rooms with heavy metal doors, which had small slots where windows should be to see in and hear what was going on. There was also a slotted tiny door further down, where it looked like things could be handed in.

My legs nearly buckled beneath me. My heart skittered out of control. Crap. I felt like I might puke at any moment. This is where they housed criminals. Like actual hardened criminals, and I was stuck here.

We were brought over to booking where correction officers sat ready to log our information and double check what had been on our persons when we came in. Apparently, our belongings would be put in a locker, and we'd get them when and if we were released.

It took about forty-five minutes for everything—my mug shot, fingerprints, my personal data being uploaded onto their system. I'd now and forever have a record.

"Alright, ladies, follow me. You're going to be in Tank One. There's a phone in there, so if you need to make a call, now's the time to do it."

"Can we bond out?" I asked, not that I had any of my credit cards or debit cards on me at the moment, and even if I did, they were now tucked away with the rest of my belongings.

"I told you when we were processing you, your bond is twenty-five hundred dollars." The officer seemed annoyed.

"Sorry, I must have missed that." For shit's sake, it wasn't like I got arrested all the time. I'd been freaking out since the cops first stepped foot into the bar. My mind couldn't keep up with everything around me.

Once we stepped into the "tank," which consisted of a smallish room, a metal toilet against the back wall, a phone near the front, and a few mattresses on the floor, I nearly lost all the contents of my stomach.

A thin woman with long, greasy blonde hair glowered at us. "Stop looking at me, bitch."

My head spun back to face the door that'd just slammed shut behind us. Crap.

"Do you know who I am?" the lady asked. She started howling and trying to climb up the wall.

"Sweet Jesus," Maude said. "What the hell is wrong with her?"

"Don't say it too loud. She might kill us," I whispered.

"I'd like to see her try."

"Well, I wouldn't." I leaned against the wall, the sudden urge to pee coming over me. But there's no way I wanted to use the bathroom in front of everyone.

"Keep it down in there," one of the officers yelled at the lady through the slotted window.

"Wolves can howl if they want," the woman spat back.

"I'm going to try to call Sophie." Kerrie hurried to the phone while trying to avoid the woman at the center of the cell. "Sophie, it's Mom. Please pick up. Hey, yeah, I-I'm not going to make it home tonight. No, that recording was a joke. I'm not really in jail." She gave a fake laugh, her eyes wide as she met my gaze. "Can you call Dad to tell him you guys will need a ride to school?"

Kerrie's shoulders hunched. I felt bad for her. I knew her kids counted on her.

"No, I'm not with a guy, either. I'm with some friends from work. One of them had a really bad break up and needs me." She paused again. "Even if I was spending the night with a man, I wouldn't tell you."

From where I stood, I heard Sophie laugh. "Whatever, Mom. Enjoy yourself."

When Kerrie hung up, she came over to stand next to me. "H-how are we going to get out of here?"

"I'm trying to think of someone to call for bond. Whoever it is, I can pay them back tomorrow," I said.

Getting ahold of my stepdad was out of the question. He'd probably call my mom, and I'd never hear the end of it. Shit. But on the other hand, I didn't want to spend the night with werewolf girl howling in the cell.

"All our bonds are twenty-five hundred, right?" I glanced at the other two.

"Yes, but that's triple someone would have to come up with. I don't have anyone I can call. Damn Corny for leaving me." Maude shook her head in dismay, tapping her heel on the floor.

"I-I have some money in my savings I could pay someone back with. It means I won't be able to move out of the house for a while, but it's better than being stuck in here."

I groaned. Who could I call?

Wooyoung! Of course. He knew all three of us. But did he have that kind of money laying around? Damn it. When we'd gone on our first date, he'd talked about having to bail his ex out of jail. Would he think I was just like her? The only other option would be to sit overnight and wait to be arraigned in front of a judge, which I definitely didn't want to do.

"Let me call Wooyoung."

"Do you know his number?" Kerrie clutched my arm, hope filling her tear-filled eyes.

My face flushed. "Yes, I memorized it after our first date."

Hopefully he picked up. It was getting super late. A recording came on for me to say my name. A second later, I heard Wooyoung's voice.

"Piper? Why are you calling me collect from jail?"

"Oh, my God. It's a long story, but I have a huge favor to ask. Maude, Kerrie, and I got arrested tonight for disorderly conduct when we went out for a drink. There was this guy who grabbed Maude, then all kinds of hell broke loose," I said in a flurry of words. "Is there any way you can come bond us out? We can all pay you back tomorrow. I'll even throw in interest."

The howling lady stopped trying to climb the wall and fell to her knees on all fours and started to bark, a puddle beneath her.

She'd pissed on the floor.

"What is that noise? Are you guys okay?"

"It's some crazy lady that's in the cell with us. I know we've only been dating for a short time, but I swear, I'll pay you back if you can do this."

"How much?"

"For all three of us, it's seventy-five hundred."

I waited for him to say no, but he was quiet for a long moment instead.

"Okay. I'll be down there as soon as I can."

"I could kiss you right now. Thank you. I owe you big time." My voice cracked with emotion. "I promise, I'll make this up to you."

"I'm not asking you to."

"I know." But there weren't too many people I knew who would drop that kind of money to bond three women out of jail.

"I'll see you soon, Piper."

When I hung up, tears fell from my lashes. "He's going to come bond us out."

"Thank goodness! You better hang on to him," Maude said. "Not every man would do something like that."

I smiled. "I know, but do you guys realize how embarrassing this is?"

"Tell me about it," Kerrie said. "Demarcus was just starting to take an interest in me, but I doubt he's going to ask me on a date after this charade. I wish the floor would swallow me up."

"Well, who knows, maybe he likes a girl in handcuffs," I teased.

She groaned. "Not helping."

As we were being out-processed, Griff, Sal, and Tony also got bonded. We stood together, all of us waiting our turn.

Griff cleared his throat and faced Maude. "Look, I really didn't mean to grope you. Believe me or not. However, I'd like to make a proposition that none of us file assault charges."

Maude frowned. "What do you mean?"

"I know I accidentally grabbed you. But what about your friends? Sal wasn't the first to throw a punch back at the bar." He glanced at me.

My nose wrinkled. "He's right, I did throw the first punch at him."

"None of us need charges on our record." Maude sighed. "Fine. I agree, but if you ever touch me like that I again, I will not hold back my wrath."

It took us about two hours to get released. Wooyoung posted our bond, then we were given appearance dates for court.

"Do you guys just want to crash at my place tonight since it's so late?" Wooyoung asked from the driver's seat.

"If that's what's easiest," Maude said with a yawn. "My old body can't handle too many of these late nights."

"Yeah, I already told Sophie I wouldn't be home until tomorrow. I don't want to scare everyone by walking in in the middle of the night," Kerrie agreed.

My hand found Wooyoung's, and I gave it a squeeze. "I'm fine with that. Do you have enough room for all of us?"

"If you're fine sharing a room with me, then Maude and Kerrie can use the guest room which has two double beds."

My pulse raced, even if I was fatigued. The idea of falling asleep next to Wooyoung still made me giddy.

"Okay."

When we got to his apartment, Wooyoung showed everyone where things were at. I followed him upstairs, kicking my shoes off near his closet.

"Do you want something else to sleep in?" He gestured to my jeans.

"If you don't mind. Also, I'm going to use the bathroom. I was too scared to use the toilet in the cell."

He chuckled. "I never imagined hearing those words come from your mouth."

I flushed. "Me, either. But thank you for being so understanding. I know your ex put you through a lot, so the fact that you came to our rescue, no questions asked, is amazing."

He handed me one of his t-shirts and a pair of long flannel pajama pants with a string. "I like you, and I know you're not the type of girl to get in trouble with the law. And if I ever meet this Griff guy or his son, I might sock them in the jaw myself. Why didn't any of you press assault charges?"

"Er...because then we'd all have had that charge. I gave Sal a bloody nose, Maude hit Griff, so we all decided, collectively between the guys and girls, not to pursue that."

He shook his head. "Go on and get changed. Do you want anything to eat or drink before bed?"

I glanced at the clock on the nightstand. It was already after three in the morning. "No, I'm good."

I went into his bathroom and slid out of my clothes. After relieving myself, I washed my hands and tugged his t-shirt over my head. The flannel pants were super long, so I decided to forgo them and just wear the shirt.

When I came out, Wooyoung stood shirtless in a pair of jogging shorts. I swallowed hard. His six pack had me daydreaming of things I'd like to do him. For starters, running my hands along the contoured muscles and working their way down.

Crap. Sharing a bed with him tonight would definitely be difficult. My eyes trailed over him until our gazes clashed.

"You ready for bed now?" he asked, his voice hoarse.

"Yes."

I set my things on top of his dresser, then climbed into bed. He situated himself next to me, then he flipped off the bedside lamp.

He scooted closer until his hand cupped my face. "Try and get some sleep, Piper."

"I will." My lips brushed against his. Heart thrashing, I snuggled against him as his arm wrapped around my waist.

"Goodnight," I said.

"Goodnight. I know it's kind of soon in our relationship, and I don't expect you to say it back yet, but I'm falling for you, Piper. I just felt like you should know."

The 'L' word. Something I didn't think anyone would ever say to me again. Not that he actually said it yet. He was right, I wasn't ready to say it back yet. But maybe soon.

I caressed his cheek, then closed my eyes. "Do you think Mr. Dancy would be mad if we all called to say we're going to be late tomorrow?"

Wooyoung's chest vibrated against me with a laugh. "Probably, but it's fine. I'll tell him you guys had an emergency and I had to help you. No worries."

No worries. Was there any such thing? "Let's just hope he doesn't find out his greeting card staff went to jail."

"I'm sure he won't." After a long silence and with hesitation in his voice, he spoke into my hair. "Also, I wondered if you might like to meet my parents someday soon?" This was followed by another bout of silence, and a slight shift in the bed. "I've told them a lot about you, and they'd like you to come to dinner so they can get to know you."

Meeting parents was a big deal. Was it too soon? I mean, we'd only been dating about a month. Although, in that time, he'd already bailed me out of jail and saved me from my ex. Even if I wasn't one hundred percent sure, I was ready.

"Sure, just let me know when."

Chapter Fourteen

KERRIE

I awoke the next morning in a bed that wasn't my own, sunlight streaming in like a laser light show. For a moment, I basked in the warmth of the comforter, then last night came crashing in on me all at once.

Bar fight.

Jail.

Bond money.

Sitting up suddenly, my head throbbed. I'd never, in all my forty plus years, ever been in trouble with the law. What if Hal found out what'd happened? Would he use it against me to go for custody of the kids? My stomach knotted at the thought. Why hadn't I contained myself last night?

Because you're a decent person who didn't want to watch your friend get groped.

Maude stirred in the bed beside mine, her eyes finally flicking open. "Ah, too much light. My head is pounding."

"I don't think the light is the reason." I tossed back my blankets, still wearing last night's clothes. "Probably those drinks you downed like they were going out of style."

"Shh. Use your indoor voice." She pulled her arms over her face as if that would shield her from any noise.

"Funny, you sound like me talking to my kids."

"I suppose I ought to get up." Her white hair stood on end like someone had ripped the stuffing out of a pillow or plush toy. Somehow, she still had lipstick on.

"Yeah, we've already overslept for work." With a yawn, I made my way to the bathroom.

Once everyone was up, Maude called in late for all of us. We figured Mr. Dancy had the most tolerance for her. She'd made up some excuse about Piper, Wooyoung, and I going to help her with her vehicle, which I had no idea if he believed or not. But at least I was beyond my probationary period, so even if he didn't, I hoped my job would be safe.

Wooyoung dropped Maude off first, then took me to get my van from the bar parking lot. I figured he wanted a few extra minutes with Piper, since it would've made more sense for him to drop her off first because she lived closest to him. They were in that new romance stage where they couldn't get enough of one another, hence the drop off order.

"I'll stop on my way back to work to get money from my savings," I said, as I got out of his vehicle. "See you guys at the office."

Once seat-belted into my van, I rested my head against the headrest. The bond money. Damn, that was going to hurt. Not to mention, it meant a prolonged stay with Hal until I could sock away more of my checks. My hands tightened on the steering wheel. I just wanted to move on and find happiness. To provide my kids with a loving home where I didn't have to worry about strange women being in my house or random fights with Hal.

By the time I got back to my house, my nerves were frazzled playing through every scenario in regard to people finding out about my stint in jail. Not that I was a hardened criminal, but it was embarrassing.

Hal met me at the door. "Why the hell did you stay out all night? You were supposed to be here after work to be with the kids. I had to cancel plans."

I snorted, dropping my purse on the counter. "Well, boo freaking hoo. Why is it okay for you to leave for days on end and sleep with God only knows how many women, but it's not alright for me to have one night out with the girls? I'm tired of the double standard, Hal. You want our divorce to be top secret, however, you want the perks of me taking care of everything. And need I add, you don't even bother calling to check in on our kids when you're gone?"

"You've never done stuff like this before. When we were married, you were never interested in going out, not with me, or any friends."

"Because you never asked. You worked, and on occasion, you'd have sex with me. But it was always *what's for dinner? Can you tell the kids to quiet down?* Never a *hey, I love you, what do you say we go get food tonight so you don't have to cook?*"

He frowned, running a hand through his hair. "Let's not get into this now. I'm going to be out of town for a few days. So, you'll need to make sure you're here for the kids."

"Other than last night, aren't I always? They're my life, Hal, and they should be yours, too. And by the way, I have a work retreat in a couple of weeks. It's mandatory, so you'll need to plan on being here."

"Fine. Tell the kids I'll see them soon."

"Or you could call them tonight. You know, try and be a parent."

He didn't respond, rather, he grabbed his duffel bag and headed out the door.

"Damn it!" I shouted when he drove off. Typical Hal fashion, always leaving. It's what he did best. How had I ever even fallen for him?

Then I remembered how much I used to make him smile. Those first dates in college where he brought me flowers or bought me dinner because I was too busy studying to leave my dorms. He'd been so patient with me back then, waiting until I was ready to have sex, never pushing. Although, given our recent history, I wondered if he'd cheated back then.

I chewed my bottom lip. Was our whole relationship a farce? Had he ever truly been in love with me? A part of me wanted to ask him, but the other part was chicken. Not that any of it mattered now. We were divorced. Done. Finished. And I'd never take him back, even if he begged and pleaded with me. Which I knew he'd never do. He'd found what he was searching for, and it wasn't me.

With a sigh, I grabbed my phone from my purse and pulled up my contacts.

Me: *Hey, Soph, just wanted to tell you I'm sorry I wasn't home last night.*

Sophie: *It's fine, Mom. Besides, you deserve a break every now and then. No worries.*

Me: *I'll be here tonight. We can have homemade pizza, maybe watch some shows as a family.*

Sophie: *You mean a family minus Dad?*

Me: *Yes. Aren't you in class?*

Sophie: *Just starting third hour. Will talk to you tonight.*

I clicked out of our conversation, not wanting to get her in trouble, then saw the last message I'd had from Demarcus. Oh, God. I'd almost forgotten about the embarrassment of him arresting us last night.

My eyes welled. We'd really hit it off, but after this, I might as well kiss that potential boyfriend goodbye. Not that I needed a man at the moment. There were so many things I had on my plate right now. The court hearing coming up. The retreat. School would be ending for the kids soon, so I'd have to get things figured out for them to have activities to do this summer. Sophie already agreed to watch them. I offered to pay her a little bit, and to also see if my ex in-laws might be willing to take the youngest two once a week, so Sophie could enjoy some down time, too. She'd be going into her senior year this upcoming school year, which also meant I needed to set aside money for pictures and graduation stuff.

"Okay, take a deep breath. Don't worry about things that haven't happened yet."

However, it was easier said than done.

After a long shower, I finally got dressed and drove into work. Hopefully, Mr. Dancy wouldn't be too ticked off at me. The first people I saw when I walked in were Piper and Wooyoung, who stood only inches apart. Even from here, I sensed the spark between them.

Piper glanced up. "Hey, you made it."

"How's the boss acting?" My fingers gripped my purse strap.

"Not sure yet, I haven't seen him. I think he's in his office. So, I'm going to quit talking and get to work so he isn't reminded we're late." She smiled, hurrying down the hall.

I scurried after her. No need to be a blip on Mr. Dancy's radar. As if sensing our thoughts, he appeared just in front of us. He crossed his arms over his chest, but didn't say anything as Maude came bursting in the front entrance as well.

"Don't worry, I'm here, Mr. Dancy. Car's working better now. Not having Corny around is a real pisser, I tell you." Maude lied without cracking a smile. I had to give it to her, she was good.

Mr. Dancy's eyes softened, or maybe that was the heat of the building melting them. Either way, I hoped Mr. Dancy didn't see through this, or we might all get canned.

Chapter Fifteen
MAUDE

Mr. Dancy followed me into my office after my 'car's broke' lie. Sometimes the man was way too nosy for his own good. When we got inside, he shut the door behind him.

"Tell me, Maude, did you really have car troubles?" He crossed his arms over his chest again, gaze narrowed in on me like he was Columbo or something.

"Yes. You know I'm always here on time."

"Hmm. We used to be comrades in arms here. The old folks sticking together. What happened?"

"Corny left me, that's what happened. Now, I'm going to live life on my terms. Besides, I can't always be a stick in the mud. There are so many things I still want to do."

He gripped my desk chair. "Wait, you're not retiring, are you?"

"Jesus H. Christ, no. Here's the thing, I'm not getting any younger. I've always been such a stickler for rules and taking the route of straight and narrow. But now, I want to live a little, maybe try some things I've never done before."

"Like be late for work?"

I snorted. "Honestly, is that all you think about? Work?"

"When you run a business for as long as I have, yes, that's all you think about. No time for other stuff."

"Sounds like you should take a vacation." I set my purse and thermos of coffee on the edge of my desk. "Your wife would probably love it if you surprised her with a trip."

He chuckled. "Or she'd think my body had been taken over by aliens."

We all already thought that, but no need to tell Mr. Boss Man. "I should get to work. These cards aren't going to write themselves."

"Right. See you later, Maude."

I gave him a mock salute, then plopped in my chair. Phew, that man and all his questions.

By some miracle, I got a few lines typed up for a new card idea. Better than what I'd been able to do lately, so I'd call that a win. Grabbing my lunch, I headed to the cafeteria where I spotted Carlos sitting at a table by himself. His facial hair still hadn't been shaved recently, and his normally pressed pants looked as if he'd pulled them out of the laundry hamper ten minutes before he came to work.

"Mind if I sit with you?" I asked.

He shrugged, scooting to make room for me. Carlos ran a hand through his already unruly dark hair.

"I think I owe you an apology about that whole penis thing. You see, Corny left me around that time, and I couldn't tolerate being around men."

"It's okay, I understand." He gave me a sad smile.

I sat beside him and took out a turkey sandwich. "How are you doing?"

Carlos sighed, using his fork to push salad around his plate. "Been better. I'm not sure whether to be sad, or angry, or relieved about Pietro leaving me. We were together for such a long time, so to have him just up and go to France without any warning…"

He stabbed a tomato as if he were after someone in a horror movie.

"Well, let me say this—I think you're better off without him. You don't want to be with someone who doesn't love you the same way you love them. Take whatever time you need to try and get over him. But then, let him go. Life's too short to be wasting tears on the likes of him."

"You're right, of course." Carlos grinned. "If he doesn't recognize how wonderful I am, then screw him."

"Cheers!" I raised my bottle of water.

"What are we giving cheers for?" Piper asked, coming to sit with us, along with Kerrie.

"For Carlos to move on from Pietro—that no good bastard who left him."

"Ah, let me raise a glass, too!" She reached for her iced tea and held it up.

"Hear, Hear," Kerrie said, plopping down across from Carlos.

"Carlos, you know what you should do? Get jazzed up tonight and come out to get a bite to eat with me."

"Really?"

"Yes. I think you need a distraction, and a night on the town will do you some good," I said. "Do they even say night on the town anymore?" My gaze met Piper's.

"No offense, but no, they don't."

I rolled my eyes. Geesh, I couldn't keep up with the times. "Either way, we should go somewhere for food and maybe a drink."

"I know just the place." Carlos's whole face lit up like the Chicago cityscape at night.

"What about you two? Are you in?" I turned to Piper and Kerrie.

Piper held up her hands. "Oh, no. Not after last night. That was a little *too* adventurous for me."

"Same. I'll have to pass for tonight, but maybe we can grab take-out after work sometime and go to the beach or park or one of our houses," Kerrie added.

Carlos glanced between us. "What happened last night?"

Did I detect a note of worry in his voice? "Nothing you need to worry about. It's all in the past."

"Damn, now you have me kind of freaked out, chica." Carlos stared at the other two as if hoping they might spill the beans, but they kept quiet, likely because they were scared Mr. Dancy would find out the real reason we were all late today.

"I promise, I'll be on my best behavior tonight." I raised my hand in a sort of salute.

"Okay then. Why don't you give me your address, and I'll pick you up around seven." He typed my information into his phone, then headed for the cafeteria exit. "You, Maude, are going to be in for the time of your life tonight."

"Can't wait!" Sweet Jesus, I hoped I didn't regret this.

When he left, I turned to the other two. "Are you chickens? Can't you see that poor Carlos needs us?"

"I know, I know. But I really don't want to get into any more trouble, especially since Hal could use last night against me," Kerrie said. "And I have the kids at home. Their dad is already gone half the time. I don't want to be absent, too."

I nodded. "You're right, you should be home with your children. Piper?"

She flushed. "I'm supposed to go over to Wooyoung's for dinner and a movie, but maybe I could convince him to come out with us, too."

"That would be nice if you can. Call and let me know for sure. The more, the merrier," I said.

"I can ask him now, before he gets back to his office," she said, leaving her food on the table and heading over to his.

"I feel like we've started an office support group, of sorts." Kerrie peered at me between bites of her sandwich.

"Complete with jail time, fighting, and lying to our boss." I laughed.

"Did you say lying to your boss?" Mr. Dancy appeared out of nowhere, standing on the other side of the table.

Good grief, he was like a genie, poofing here and there with no warning. About enough to give an old gal a heart attack.

"No. You misheard. I said, 'crying to our boss.' As in, all of us have been in dire straits lately, and you've been very compassionate." Hells bells, the one time I'm not careful.

"Did you also mention jail?" He crossed his arms.

"Mr. Dancy, no offense, but you might need to look into hearing aids. I get a lot of those pamphlet things in the mail, maybe I should bring you one. What I said was 'complete with nails and moonlighting.' We went to get our nails done last night, then headed to the beach to watch the sunset and the moon rise."

"Oh. That makes more sense. Carry on," he said. As he walked away, I watched him stick his finger in his ear as if to clean it out.

"That was close," I whispered. "Gotta be more careful with Boss Man around."

"No kidding. I about had a panic attack when he showed up." Kerrie took several deep breaths, her hand rested against her chest.

Piper came back and sat down again. "Wooyoung said he's game for dinner tonight. We'll meet up at your house at around seven."

"Sounds good. I'll let Carlos know in case he needs to make reservations." I stood, picking up my trash. "See you later."

Carlos was, of course, happy we'd have additional guests coming along. "I can't wait for you to experience this. It's like dinner and a show."

"Oh, should I dress up?"

"Only if you want to. I'll pick you all up after work." Carlos grinned, hurrying back to his office.

⪻

"Do you know where we're going?" Piper asked as we sat on the porch, waiting for Carlos.

"No. He only said it was dinner and a show, so it could be anywhere."

"I wonder if it's that medieval dinner place?" Wooyoung stood with his hands in his pockets, his polo shirt tight across his muscular chest.

Piper couldn't take her eyes off him, and I could see why. I might be old, but I wasn't dead.

"He didn't say, but I'm game for anything." I smoothed my black skirt, which I accompanied with a pink dress shirt and pink heels.

A few minutes later, Carlos pulled up in a gray SUV.

"Hey, guys." He waved, hopping out to open the doors for us. His dark hair was tamed tonight and styled off his face. He wore a dark polo shirt over a pair of tight jeans. He'd even shaved his face, looking more Carlos-like than he had in weeks. "We're going to have so much fun."

"Where exactly are we going?" My gaze met his.

"It's a surprise, but I'll tell you they have the best burgers in all Chicago, chica."

"Burgers sound good, I'm starving," Piper said.

We drove across town and parked outside of a place called Happy's Handsome Hamburgers. Couldn't go wrong with a name like that.

Carlos came around and got my door for me, while Wooyoung did the same for Piper. We walked toward the entrance. I'm not sure what I expected, but it sure wasn't what I got when the door opened to reveal a dimly lit restaurant with a stage at the front, and Drag Queens doing a dance.

"Wow, I'll admit, this is a first for me," I said, as a tall queen with ebony skin and long braids swept past me, carrying a tray with food on it. "They perform and also serve food?"

"Well, they have some that are specifically the wait staff, and others who are strictly performers. But for certain numbers, all of them stop what they're doing and dance."

"Oh." I caught Piper's eye, and she grinned.

"This is so cool. I've never been to a drag show before." Her gaze scoured the room as if taking it all in.

"How many tonight?" A tiny redhead came up to us, wearing a short, tight black number.

"Four," Carlos answered for us.

Once we were seated, we were handed menus.

"What's on the Ride 'em Cowboy Burger?" I asked, squinting at the small print.

"Pretty much all the fixings," Carlos said. "They're super yummy."

I followed his gaze to the stage and wondered if he was talking about the food or the show about to start.

"Alright, I'll get me one of those, then."

After we all ordered, the stage lit with several lights and queens in every shape, color, and size.

"The one on the end, Juanita, is my best friend."

Piper turned her head to see where he pointed. "Oh, my God, his makeup is amazing. And his legs. Holy shit, I'd kill to have legs that long. Wait, does he go by he or she?"

"Juanita goes by he. He's actually Juan the accountant by day, and Juanita the show girl by night. Some of the queens have undergone surgery and recognize as women, but others, like Juanita, just dress the part."

"Whoa, if I kicked my leg that high, I'd likely throw out my hip." I watched them do a variety of complicated dance steps before Juanita took the microphone and began to sing. "Say, what do they do with their willies?"

Carlos chuckled. "Girl, they ice 'em and tuck 'em. Although, like I said, some have undergone surgery."

"Oh, that doesn't seem like it'd be too comfortable."

After several numbers, Juanita hopped off the stage and made a beeline for our table. He stopped, hand on his hip, his long dark wig hanging to the middle of his back. He wore a tight red dress that came down to his thighs, topped off with a pair of three-inch spiky red heels. His brown eyes rested on Carlos.

"Bitch, about time you showed up. I can't believe you've been avoiding me. Although..." His gaze flitted over to Wooyoung. "If this is your new man, I can see why."

Wooyoung's face turned the color of a fire engine.

"Sassy as ever, I see. And no, sadly, Wooyoung is with Piper. Maude is my date tonight."

Carlos slipped his arm around my shoulders.

"Well now, I've really been out of the loop for a while if you're spicing things up in this way. Good on you finding a beautiful sugar mama." Juanita touched my shoulder, giving it a slight squeeze.

"Maude is simply a lifesaver, darling. I promise that I'm now officially over Pietro." Carlos lifted his margarita and took a sip.

"Hell, yes. Finally. I don't know what magic you used, Maude, but thank you. I've been trying to get this man out of his house for weeks now."

"Must be all my sugar." I laughed.

"Okay, this is going to seem like an absurd question, but can I please get tips on makeup from you? Your eyeshadow is freaking out of this world," Piper said, setting her pop down on the table.

"Of course." Juanita fluffed his hair. "I've got another number coming up in a few, but if you give Carlos your contact information, I'd be glad to meet up with you or talk you through it."

"You are awesome, thank you."

"No problem, love. Any friend of Carlos's is a friend of mine. Now, I must go." He spun dramatically and raced for the stage just as the music started again.

We watched several performers, and they were amazing. Never in all my seventy plus years did I think I'd find myself here.

When Carlos brought us back to my house, I waved goodnight to everyone.

The buttery yellow of my porchlight welcomed me home, but as soon as I unlocked the door, the silence surrounded me, reminding me again Corny wasn't here. I swallowed hard as I stared at a picture of him sitting on the coffee table by the couch.

"See, you lying bastard, I'm being more adventurous. Bet you never thought I'd go to a drag show or get in a bar fight. I'm doing just fine without you." My voice cracked, but I swallowed back the emotion. "Yep, just fine."

Chapter Sixteen

PIPER

"Wish me luck," I said to Kerrie and Maude as we headed to the parking lot after work. "I'm meeting Wooyoung's parents tonight, and I'm sorta freaking out."

Maude reached for my hand and gave it a squeeze. "You, my dear, will be just fine. Wooyoung's a good guy. He must really like you a lot to bring you home to his parents already."

I sighed, hoping she was right.

"What Maude said. And don't overthink this. You're an absolutely loveable person. I'm not just saying that because you're one of my best friends, either." Kerrie smiled, grabbing my other hand. "You've got this, girl! Tomorrow, we want *all* the details." She waggled her eyebrows.

I snorted. "Not sure what you think is going to happen at his family's house, but I doubt there will be anything physical."

"Oh, I don't know. I've seen those movies where the man or woman takes their significant other or suitor to their childhood home and they engage in whoopy," Maude said with a laugh. "Corny and I got a little frisky—"

"Ah, I'm stopping you right there." My eyes rolled skyward as I walked away from Maude and Kerrie. "I'll see you guys later."

"Chicken," Maude called after me.

Kerrie laughed. "Oh, to be young again."

"Ah, you're still a young girl yourself." I overheard Maude say to Kerrie. And she was right. Kerrie wasn't exactly old.

I walked back to my house to get changed, trying to determine whether I wanted to wear jeans and a nice shirt or go for something dressier like a summer dress and cardigan. God, I hated the idea of meeting parents for the first time. I'd never had to do anything like this before. What if they hated me? Or maybe they'd think I wasn't good enough for Wooyoung.

My stomach churned, and I hoped I wouldn't end up in the bathroom. Now that'd make a great first impression, blowing up their toilet. Wrinkling my nose, I continue to scour my closet as if by shifting the clothes around, a new item would appear.

"Relax. You've got this," I said, repeating Kerrie's mantra aloud before grabbing my blue, white, and yellow sundress from a hanger. I'd err on the side of dressy, but comfy.

Once I finished getting ready, I headed down to the lobby to wait for Wooyoung. I sucked in a deep breath, trying to ignore my sweaty palms. Soon, he parked in front of the building, and I hurried to meet him.

He climbed from his vehicle, his long legs tucked into a pair of loose fit jeans, his broad shoulders stretching the fabric of a thin light blue V-neck sweater. His dark eyes met mine, and I nearly puddled on the sidewalk.

"You look beautiful," he said, giving me a quick peck on the cheek before I climbed into his car.

"You aren't so bad yourself."

His gaze held mine, making me wish we could go up to my apartment instead. However, I knew this was a huge step for him to be bringing me home to his family, and our not showing up probably wouldn't earn me any points. Not that I needed them to like me, but I wanted them to.

He shut the car door and got into the driver's side. About ten minutes later, we pulled up to a three-story old brownstone. It was narrow with dark blue shutters and flower boxes beneath the lower-level windows. A small wrought iron gate separated the home from the sidewalk. A narrow driveway wrapped around the back of the house where there was just enough room for three small cars, but nothing else. No backyard to be seen, however, they did have a beautiful screened-in porch, which I assumed must've been added long after the brownstone was built.

"You ready?" Wooyoung smiled at me as we got out of the car, and he took my hand in his.

My lips turned up at the corners. "As I'll ever be."

"You'll be great. I know my parents are going to love you."

I let out a hiss of air and followed him inside. As soon as we got indoors, the scent of kimchi assaulted my nose. I'd eaten enough of it with Minho's family to recognize the smell.

We left our shoes in the entry and slid our feet into slippers that awaited us.

"Good, good, you're finally here," a short woman with shoulder-length dark hair, and a petite frame said, reaching to give Wooyoung a big squeeze.

I released his hand and stood back.

"You never come see us anymore," she said in a voice that was meant to chastise, but came out sounding more like she was teasing. Then she turned her beautiful smile on me. "You must be Piper? We've heard so much about you from Woo."

"Hi, it's good to meet you." I held my hand out in greeting.

"This is my mother, Jisoo, and my father, Jinyoung." He nodded to a tall man with the same build and facial structure as him. The only visible difference between father and son was the spattering of gray in Jinyoung's dark hair.

Jinyoung shook my hand, as well. "Welcome to our home. My wife has cooked us up a great meal tonight. We have Woo's favorite bulgogi and kimchi. I hope you're okay with that?"

"Yes, of course. I'm a huge kimchi fan."

We went into the dining room, where plates were already set out. There was a mixture of chopsticks and silverware next to each place setting, and I realized they likely did this for my benefit. Although, I definitely knew how to use chopsticks, but I still appreciated they thought of me.

"Everything smells and looks so good," I said as Wooyoung came around and ushered me into a chair. He took the one next to mine, his gaze beaming.

"So, Wooyoung told us you're a writer at the card company?" Jisoo reached over to grab my bowl, adding some kimchi to it.

"Yes. It's a fun job, most of the time." I laughed, trying not to dwell on the fact that there'd been a period of time it hadn't been. But I wasn't going to rehash that. Not tonight.

My gaze fell on the extra plates and bowls. Did they always set this many places at the table?

I'd barely gotten the thought processed when I heard a door open.

"Hello, we're here. Sorry we're late," a female voice carried into the dining room.

Beside me, Wooyoung stiffened. "I thought I told you not to invite them."

"Your sister wanted to meet your girlfriend, too. Don't be such a brat." Jisoo swatted at him.

At that moment, I watched in horror as Hani and Minho walked into the room. My breath caught in my throat as I tried to figure out what was happening. Hani? She was Wooyoung's sister?

My fists tightened at my side as I met Minho's gaze. My ex had cheated on me with my current boyfriend's sister. What the actual hell? Then another thought dawned on me.

Wooyoung had known this whole time.

I swallowed past the lump in my throat, hopped to my feet, pushed past Wooyoung, who had also stood as well as Minho. "I'm sorry, I've got to go."

I slid my feet out of the slippers and back into my sandals, then grabbed my purse from a bench by the door and raced outside. Tears burned my eyes, my chest tightening. How could Wooyoung do this to me?

For shit's sake, he'd had plenty of time to tell me the truth, but he didn't.

"Piper, wait," someone called after me. Only it wasn't Wooyoung as I'd expected. Instead, I found Minho chasing after me. "You don't have to leave. Hani and I can come back another time. Stay, get to know Wooyoung's family."

I shook my head.

"Look, I didn't realize it was Wooyoung standing on your balcony that day. I never put two and two together," he rushed. "Are we really still at a point where we can't be adults and be in the same room together?"

My head snapped up, my narrowed eyes boring into his. "You don't get it, do you? You hurt me so much. Like you took my heart out and stomped on it. I mean, one second, we were engaged, planning a future together, and the next, you're fucking the florist in *our* car. How am I supposed to just get over that and pretend it didn't happen?"

He frowned, running a hand through his hair. "I'm sorry, I never meant to hurt you. You've got to believe that."

I snorted. "Hard to believe it when my last memory of you includes Hani's legs wrapped around you."

"I know I've said it before, but I'll say it again. I want us to be friends, for us to still be close."

Tears streamed down my cheeks. "That's not possible."

Wooyoung came bounding down the driveway toward us, and Minho headed back inside.

My jaw tightened as I stared at him. "You knew this whole time that your sister is the one who screwed up my relationship with Minho. Was this some sort of joke to you? I mean, asking me out and inviting me to dinner?"

He reached for me, but I pulled back.

"No, I didn't know the whole time, not until the night at the restaurant. And to answer your question, this wasn't a joke. You're not a joke. I told my mom not to invite them."

"So, what you're saying is, if they hadn't happened to show up today, I'd still not know the truth?"

"This is exactly why I didn't want to mention it. You're so hung up on your ex and what he did to you that you can't or won't see what's right in front of you. I've been trying so hard, but maybe convincing someone to love you shouldn't be this difficult." His hands shoved into his pockets as he stared at me. "I'm done trying to prove myself to you, to make you see that I'm not Minho, because I doubt you'll ever be happy."

I staggered back a step as if his words had been his hands shoving me. "Fine. If that's what you think, I'll see you at work or whatever." With a shake of my head, I glared. "You don't get it at all, do you? It's one thing to get over someone and move on, but another entirely to try and play nice with someone who's betrayed you. You're expecting way too much from me, Wooyoung. I told you at the beginning how much he hurt me. You don't understand, and likely never will."

Turning on my heel, I ambled down the sidewalk.

"Wait, at least let me drive you home," Wooyoung said, trying to play his knight in shining armor card. But it was too late for that.

"No. I'm good," I said over my shoulder. "You should go eat before everything gets cold."

"But it's too far to walk by yourself," he argued.

"I'm fine, really. I've taken care of myself this long, I'm sure I can manage to find my way home."

This time, I kept walking. A sob escaped my lips as I rounded the corner of the block, but not once did I look back. Wooyoung was like every other man I knew, other than my stepdad. A liar. I could still feel the sting of his words as if I'd been slapped.

Crying, I found a bench and sat down, then wrapped my arms around myself. This was why I didn't want to date again. Why I didn't want to give someone my heart. It gave them too much power over me to destroy me.

I fumbled to grab my phone from my purse. Who could I call? Kerrie had her kids to take care of. I knew Maude didn't like to drive at night, but honestly, she felt like my only option. My stepdad, David, probably would come to get me, but I wasn't really wanting to talk to him. Last thing I wanted him to think was that I'd turned into my mom.

At last, I dialed Maude's number. She picked up on the third ring.

"This is Maude."

"Hey, Maude. I...uh, this is Piper. I wondered if you could come get me?" I wept into the phone.

"Piper, what's wrong?"

"I, well, Wooyoung and I broke up. I'm kind of stranded right now."

"Did that bastard leave you somewhere?"

"Not exactly."

"He better not have, or so help me, he'll be missing his bits and pieces next time we meet."

I half laughed, half cried. "Let's leave his junk alone."

"So you say now. Well, kid, let me grab my keys and purse. Do you have directions for me?"

I found the street signs and let her know what crossroad section I was at. After walking her through how to put the information into the navigation system on her phone, she hung up with me, but before doing so, she assured me she'd be here soon.

True to her word, Maude drove up to the curb about fifteen minutes later. I hopped up from the bench and hurried into her car, which smelled like warm vanilla.

When I had my seatbelt on, she pulled onto the road. "Do you want to go home or back to my house?"

"Your house, if that's alright. I don't want to be alone." And I didn't want to hear Minho come back to his apartment later tonight or, for that matter, make another attempt at being friends.

God, what was up with Minho anyway? He missed me as a friend, but not a lover? Maybe I wasn't good in bed. At this thought, I slumped further into my seat, wrapping my arms around my chest. Maybe there really was something wrong with me.

We drove in silence, except for the radio playing oldies. When we got to her house, she parked in the driveway, and I followed her inside. Instantly, I felt at home. There was something warm and inviting about her house, like a warm hug after a long day.

"Why don't you have a seat in the living room. I'll make us some hot cocoa," Maude said. "Unless you need something stronger?"

"No, cocoa is fine."

Shyly, I moved into the other room, taking a seat on the couch. On the mantel above her fireplace was a picture of a much younger Maude and Cornelius. Their wedding photo. Nothing fancy, but they looked so happy. Cornelius seemed to have a constant twinkle in his eye, which the photographer captured so well. Why had he left her? They'd seemed so in love.

"I've not been strong enough to take the pictures down yet." Maude's voice cracked with emotion.

"There's nothing that says you have to," I replied. "If it makes you happy, you should leave it up."

"I'm not sure what it makes me feel." She handed me a steaming cup of cocoa and ushered me to a spot on the couch. "That's the funny thing about someone leaving you."

I nodded. "Have you been doing okay?"

She shrugged. "For the most part. Learning to do lots of things that Corny would've normally done for me. And for the things I can't do myself, I hire the neighbor kid. Enough about me, what happened tonight?"

"Betrayal, that's what happened tonight." I went on to rehash the evening's disastrous events, my ex showing up with Wooyoung's fiancé-stealing sister, Wooyoung's deception, and all the details in between.

"Jesus H. Christ. That's horrible. I thought better of Wooyoung, but apparently my good guy radar is broken."

My chest tightened. "I wish he'd have been honest with me. Then he turned this all on me, saying I was too caught up in my ex, and I never gave him a chance."

I raised the mug to my lips and took a sip.

Maude sighed. "Well, on that point, I agree with Wooyoung. You need to let Minho go. You're only making yourself miserable by clinging to the past. However, I do feel you were giving Wooyoung a chance. You've been on several dates with him now and seemed happy."

"I was. I just don't know what to do now. Do I forgive him? And even if I do, things seemed very final when I stalked off."

Maude laughed. "One thing I know, nothing is ever final until we decide it is. If you think he's worth fighting for, then fight. If what he's done is unforgiveable, then let him go and move on."

Maude was right on all accounts. Now I just needed to decide what it was I truly wanted.

"If you spend the night, I've got some outfits for work that should fit you," Maude said.

This time, I grinned. Kerrie would probably shit herself if I came in wearing Maude's powder blue suit and matching heels. This could be fun.

"Sounds good. And Maude, thank you for rescuing me tonight."

Maude patted my arm. "That's what friends are for. Besides, we all need a little rescuing sometimes."

Chapter Seventeen

KERRIE

My gaze shifted to the front door as I sat in the lobby waiting for Piper and Maude to arrive. For once, I wasn't running behind schedule. The kids didn't need lunches as it was their last day of school, and a half day to boot. Mr. Dancy had said I could leave early to pick up the youngest.

Already, I worried about daycare over the summer. Sophie said she could handle it, but I didn't think it was fair to stick the kids with her all day, every day. Hal's parents offered to take them twice a week in order to give Sophie some time to either hang out with friends or get a part-time job that actually paid something. But if it fell through, or didn't work out, I wanted to have a backup plan.

However, having to see Hal's parents more often meant more lies, and I was tired of lying to everyone. My ex had no clue how hard this was for me.

Maude walked in, followed closely by Piper. My mouth gaped at the bright powder blue pant suit Piper wore. It looked like something from Maude's closet. Upon closer inspection, I realized it was.

"Um, are you two swapping clothes now?" I asked when they joined me.

Maude laughed. "You two could use a little sprucing up. Piper here has had her eye on this outfit for a long time, ain't that right?"

Piper smiled, but the normal twinkle in her eye was gone. There were dark lines, and remnants of tears still lingering.

"Yep, I'm a sharp dressed woman now. You better watch out, world."

"Is everything okay?" I peered between them.

Maude leaned closer and said in a hushed voice, "That good-for-nothing Wooyoung broke up with *our* Piper."

My eyes widened. No way. They'd been getting on so well. "Wait, what happened? I thought you were having dinner with his family last night. Did it not go well?"

"You could say that. Apparently, Wooyoung's sister is the home-wrecker that stole Minho away. Although, I guess Minho is even more to blame since he could've broken it off with me before sleeping with her. But yeah, they showed up for dinner—one big happy freaking family."

I rubbed my neck. "Did Wooyoung know about Minho and Hani?"

"Yes, that's the shitty part. He figured it out early on and never said anything." Her voice cracked, tears forming once more.

"Ah, forget him. You can do way better," I said. "In fact, let's not talk about him for the rest of the day, or week, or hell, even year."

"That's the spirit," Maude said. "We're back to our no penises allowed rules."

The door wooshed open again, and Wooyoung came trudging in. His normally ironed shirt looked worse for wear. Even his hair was messy. Maybe Piper wasn't the only one crushed by this breakup. But either way, I'd have Piper's back.

Wooyoung swept by us without so much as a *hi, what's up*, or *screw you*. I swallowed hard, hurting for Piper. Damn it! What was wrong with him? Maybe one of us could confront him. Although, I guess that might be a bad idea if we wanted to keep our jobs.

"You don't need him," I said, loud enough I was sure he'd heard me.

Mr. Dancy came in next, his beady eyes landing on us the moment he entered. He scowled, shaking a newspaper at us. "Why are your names in the court section of the paper? I thought you said you had car trouble, not legal issues."

Maude waved her hand at him. "Oh, Mr. Dancy, these things happen. Some rude man tried to accost me." She cupped her breasts protectively to make her point. "And these two defended me."

"Defended you right into jail?" He shoved the paper under Maude's nose.

"Yep, that about sums it up. But don't worry. All charges were dropped, we've paid our fines and such, so no harm done. Now, what do you say you let us get to work?"

Mr. Dancy opened his mouth to say something else, but Maude quickly ushered us down the hall toward our offices. "Steer clear of him the rest of the day, he'll soon forget about all this nonsense. Today is electric bill delivery day."

"Lucky us," I said. "By the way, I'll miss you guys at lunch. I've got to get my kids from school today. But if you need anything, I'm only a phone call away."

"Thanks." Piper gave me a quick hug, then hurried to her office and shut the door.

Maude met my gaze. "She had a rough night. I still don't know what came over Wooyoung. I'll fill you in later on everything that went down so she doesn't have to hash through it again. This only goes to show, even the best of men can be asses."

"You'll get no argument from me." I had an asshole of my own at home, or rather, on the road or wherever he was today, but an asshole nonetheless.

My half day of crunching numbers at the office flew by, and soon I found myself parked outside the elementary school, waiting to pick up Nella and Tommy. At least, my running would cut down for a couple of months, which in turn would save on gas money.

My fingers drummed against the steering wheel when I glanced up to find Demarcus standing on the sidewalk, waiting to pick up Mya's little brother, Mackai.

My throat thickened. We hadn't seen one another since the whole bringing me to jail incident. Already, my skin heated with embarrassment.

I admired him from afar, the way his biceps flexed as he paced back and forth. Even now, he smiled that perfect, make-me-want-to-rip-his-clothes-off smile.

A tall woman with long dark braids and beautiful skin walked up to him, pressing her lips to his cheek, and gave him a hug.

My heart hammered in my chest while disappointment flooded through me. So, he'd already moved on. Or maybe he'd had her all along. I could see why. She was tall and gorgeous, and probably didn't get handcuffed to be hauled off to the slammer. Had my stint in jail ruined things for us?

A wave of nausea swept through me. They seemed super friendly. They had to have known one another a while. Even if he decided he still wanted to go out sometime, I'd have to say no, now that I knew he had someone else. I didn't want to be the other woman.

The distant bell rang from the school, and I quickly climbed from the car and went around to the passenger side so I could help Nella and Tommy in.

"Mama, look what I made," Tommy said, running full speed toward me holding up a paper bag he'd made into a dinosaur puppet.

"Wow, that is so cool. Does he roar or talk?"

Tommy let out a loud roar and laughed.

Nella came next, carrying her backpack and a book. "I got a book from my teacher to read this summer."

"So, you guys had a good last day, then?"

"Yeah," they said in unison.

"Hop in, and let's get your seatbelts on." I leaned in to help them buckle. When I turned to head back to the driver's side, Demarcus stared in my direction.

He lifted a hand and waved.

I gave a non-committal wave back. Before I hopped into my vehicle, he started toward me.

"Hey, Kerrie, it's nice to see you," he called, keeping me from making my escape.

"You mean, nice to see me not in the back of your squad car." I gave a shaky laugh.

"That, too." He grinned.

"I'm so, so sorry about that. I've never gotten in trouble like that, not until that night. I swear, it was a heat of the moment, crime of passion to protect Maude."

He chuckled. "I'm not judging. Things happen. Normally, not stuff like that, but..." Demarcus ran a hand over his head, his mahogany eyes intent on me. "I actually came over here to see if you wanted to get dinner tonight?"

Confusion swept over me. Was he serious? And what about the model-worthy lady I'd just seen him with? "Not to sound ungrateful or snarky, but um, I saw you with that other woman earlier, and I'm not one to do the whole cheating thing."

He raised his hands, waving them in front of him. "No, no, no. That's Mya's mom, my ex. We're really good friends, but definitely divorced. She's been remarried for a couple of years now. Trust me, she and I are not getting back together. That ship sailed and sank like the Titanic long ago."

"Oh." My mouth suddenly went dry. "Sorry. Well, I'll have to ask Sophie to see if she can watch the kids. Can I text you later and let you know?"

"Sure." He smiled. "If not tonight, then maybe some other night, if it works better for you."

"I'd like that. I'll see you later?"

"Most definitely." He moved back toward the sidewalk where his son came sprinting toward him.

Whoa, did he ask me on a real date? Even after my brush with the law? Either he was crazy, really into bondage, or he actually liked me.

Sophie was already at the house when I got there.

"So, how was your last day of junior year?" I asked, setting Tommy's stuff on the center island.

"Awesome. I'm now officially a senior. Can you believe it?" She giggled, brushing a strand of her dark hair from her face.

"No. You're making me feel old, kid!"

"Do I make you feel old, too?" Nella climbed up onto a stool, trying to open a pack of fruit snacks for Tommy.

"Yes, you all make me feel old." Where had the time gone? The kids were growing up so fast. After next school year, Soph would be in college. It didn't seem possible. I tried to imagine what my life would look like with her not around as much.

I swallowed a lump in my throat. It was a bit early to be crying about her going away to college, I supposed.

"Oh, Sophie, can I talk to you a second?" I nodded toward the living room.

"Sure." She followed after me, and I stood awkwardly trying to form words.

"I...um...I wondered if you might watch the kids for a bit tonight? Demarcus invited me to dinner. But if you already have plans, I can say no," I hurried to say.

Her smile widened. "Yes. Oh. My. God. This is so freaking awesome. Wait until Mya finds out our parents are dating."

"No. I mean, we're going to dinner, but I'm not sure this means we're dating at this point."

"But you like him, don't you?" Her brows raised as she watched me.

"Of course, what's not to like?"

"I knew it. You blushed so much around him when we went to the concert. Mama's got a boyfriend," she sang under her breath.

"Shh! Don't start that." I swatted at her, but couldn't help laughing, too. Just the thought of seeing Demarcus made me giddy. I hadn't felt this way in...well, a very long time.

"You go and have fun," Sophie said at last. "I'll watch Tommy and Nella. You have to promise me, though, to enjoy yourself and not be worrying about us the whole time."

"Deal."

A few hours later, I stood waiting by the front door for Demarcus. My stomach knotted. He didn't really say where we were going. Had I gotten too dressed up? I smoothed the skirt of my black dress with sweaty palms. Little black dresses were supposed to be universal as far as dates went, right? It'd been years since I'd been on a date. I had no idea what the expectations were or any of that stuff.

I raised my hand to my mouth and did a quick breath check. Still minty fresh.

"Mom, you okay? You look like you might hurl," Sophie asked.

I gave a nervous chuckle. "I'm fine. It's just been a while since I've done this."

She nodded. "You'll be fine. It's only dinner."

Right. Only dinner. A moment later, Demarcus pulled into our driveway.

"I'll see you later. Call me if you need me."

She rolled her eyes. "We'll be fine. Go. Have fun. But not too much fun." Sophie waggled her brows.

When I got outside, Demarcus smiled. "Finally, our schedules match up for us to grab a bite." He opened the door to his SUV for me.

"Sophie was more than willing to watch the younger two," I said. "She practically shoved me out the door."

He chuckled. "Mya was pretty enthusiastic about us going on a date, too. I'm starting to wonder if they planned on us meeting up at the concert from the get-go."

"You don't think your son would pretend to be sick, do you?" I slid into the passenger side of the vehicle.

He snorted. "He'd do anything Mya asked, if she paid him. Trust me, my boy is corrupt."

We laughed. "Kids, I tell you."

"You're preaching to the choir. Some days, I'm not sure if I should be encouraging their antics, grounding them, or throwing up the white flag of surrender." He was quiet for a second before glancing over at me. "So, how have you been?"

"Hanging in there. I want to say, for the record, I'm overjoyed it's the end of the school year. It'll be a heck of a lot less running for me or helping with math homework that takes a mathematician to understand."

"I hear you. Even if I'm only doing it part of the time, it gets to be a lot."

"I'm hoping in the next few months to finally have enough saved up to move out," I said, toying with the handle of my purse.

"Do you know what area you're looking to move? I can keep an eye out for any rentals near me."

"Trying to stay in the school district, so it's a pretty decent span of area."

"Alright, I'll let you know if I hear about anything." His hands tightened on the steering wheel as he turned the corner.

We drove across town to a steakhouse I'd never been to before. When he parked, he shut the engine off. "I probably should've asked ahead of time if you're okay with steak."

"Steak is a rare thing in my house, no pun intended," I said. "And yes, I love it."

"Good, a woman after my own heart."

The aroma of beef and potatoes wafted in the air around us, and my mouth watered. It'd been a while since I'd eaten something I didn't have to cook myself.

"How many?" the hostess asked.

"Two." Demarcus reached for my hand, and in the instant our skin touched, a searing fire scorched its way right through me. If he kept this up, I might combust right out of my Spanx.

I clung tight to him as we followed the hostess to a dimly lit table in the middle of the restaurant.

"Is this okay?" She stopped to look at us.

"It's perfect," I said before casting a glance at Demarcus, who nodded his approval, as well.

"Great, go ahead and have a seat. Someone will be with you shortly to take your order."

Stained glass chandeliers with western scenes hung over the table while a condiments holder made of horseshoes sat neatly in the center.

Demarcus released my hand as we sat across from one another. "Order whatever you want. Tonight is your night to be spoiled."

"Thank you." Hal never did stuff like this for me. It was always 'watch what you order' or 'you're probably not going to eat the whole thing, so let's not waste the money.'

After scouring the menu, I decided on smothered chicken, a baked potato, broccoli, and a side salad. We placed our order, then sat waiting.

"In a couple of months, Mya asked me to take her to look at a few universities and colleges. If Sophie wants, she can tag along. I think the girls were interested in the same ones."

"That would great. If I can get time off, would you mind me riding along?" My eyes shifted to meet his.

He reached across the table, his fingers entwining with mine again. "Of course. Besides, I think I'll need parental back up. You know how those two get when they're together."

My gaze traveled over his soft lips to his neck, where his dark blue polo shirt was unbuttoned to reveal a white t-shirt beneath. I admired his biceps, and the smoothness of his hand against my own.

Did Demarcus have no flaws?

When dinner arrived, we both grew quiet, cutting into our meat. Tonight was exactly what I needed. Demarcus put me at ease with a single glance. There was just something about him.

We'd almost finished our food when my cell rang.

"Sorry," I said, grabbing it from my purse. "Hey, Soph, what's up?"

"Mom!" she cried. In the background was screaming.

"What's going on? Is everyone okay?"

"N-no. Tommy fell down the stairs. He's bleeding, and his arm is in a weird position. I tried calling Dad, but he wouldn't answer. I didn't know what to do, so I called 911, and they're sending an ambulance."

"Okay, we'll get the bill and meet you at the hospital."

"If I ride in the ambulance, then who will watch Nella?' Sophie's voice cracked.

"Call Grandma and Grandpa Holloway, and have them come down to stay will Nell."

"I will. Sorry, Mom."

"Oh, honey, it's not your fault. We'll be there as soon as we can."

When I hung up, Demarcus had already asked for the bill and was in the process of paying it.

"Tommy fell down the stairs." Tears sprung to my own eyes. "Sophie said he's bleeding, and something is wrong with his arm."

"I'll get you over to the hospital. We'll likely beat the ambulance there."

"Thank you. I'm so sorry."

He wrapped an arm around my shoulders. "Don't ever apologize for wanting to take care of your kids, Kerrie. We can have dinner together another time."

Demarcus got us across town in record time. I was thankful he knew the streets as well as he did, or we likely wouldn't have gotten there as quickly.

I waited in the ER lobby for about ten minutes before Tommy and Sophie arrived, at which time, I went back into one of the rooms with Tommy while Demarcus and Sophie stayed in the lobby.

"Mama," Tommy cried, his mouth, chin, and t-shirt stained with blood.

"Shh, it's alright. I'm here now."

A nurse came in with a doctor in tow. They took vitals and checked him over, asking me his medical history in the process.

"He'll definitely need a few stitches in his lip, and we should get an x-ray of his arm, which I'm going to say now is probably broken. We just need to see the severity of the fracture to determine what our next step is."

"Okay. Thank you."

I waited in the small room while they wheeled Tommy out for x-rays. Down the hall was the constant beeping of machines and the idle chatter from nurses and doctors.

I chewed my bottom lip, tiredness washing over me. I dialed Hal's number, and it went straight to voicemail. Christ, why wasn't he answering?

"Hal, it's Kerrie. Tommy's in the hospital. Give me call when you get this message."

Of course, absent again.

After three hours in the ER, Tommy was discharged and wheeled to the lobby, where we met up with Sophie and Demarcus.

"Is everything okay?" Demarcus rose.

"Yeah. He had to get five stitches in his lip, and he'll be in a cast for the next six to eight weeks while his arm heals."

"Ugh, thank God. I'm so sorry, Mom. I should've stopped him and Nella when they started fighting over the boardgame. They were tugging on it. I didn't think one of them would fall." Her eyes welled.

"It's okay, it's not your fault, sweetheart. Tommy and Nella fight no matter who's watching them." I hugged her, and she wrapped her arms around my waist. "Did your dad ever call you back?"

"No." She frowned. "He's such a piece of—"

"Soph."

"I know, I know. He's my dad. But he is a piece of shit. Excuse my language." Sophie glanced at Demarcus.

He chuckled. "Trust me, I've heard way worse."

Demarcus ushered us to his car, and helped me get Tommy situated. At last, we headed home.

"Thanks for the ride," I said when we got to the house.

"Anytime. I'll see you around. Maybe get raincheck on dinner?"

"I'd like that." With the kids standing there, I gave his hand a squeeze, forgoing a kiss goodnight.

We waved to him, then headed inside, where we were met by Hal's parents.

"Thank goodness he's okay!" Mrs. Holloway said. "We still haven't heard from Hal. He never answered his calls."

"I have no idea what's going on with him," I said, suddenly feeling drained. "Hey, Soph, can you bring the younger kids upstairs and help them get ready for bed?"

"Yeah, sure." She gave me a quick hug as she ushered them past. "Goodnight, Grandma and Grandpa."

"Goodnight," they called in unison.

"Thanks kiddo!" I turned back to my in-laws.

"Kerrie, he's not been around much lately. Is something going on?" My mother-in-law met my gaze.

I couldn't keep up the charade. Exhaustion set in, and before I knew it, words were pouring from my mouth. "No, it's not. He divorced me. I'm staying here until I can afford to move out." I rattled on about his not wanting anyone to know, and I suddenly felt a huge pressure lift from my shoulders. "He thought you'd be mad."

"Well, he's right. He'll get an earful when he calls, that much I can promise." My ex father-in-law pulled me in for a hug, apologizing for his son's actions, and I let myself cry because, while I no longer loved Hal, I still loved his family. But what more was there to say? At least, they knew the truth now.

And I no longer carried the burden of the lie.

Chapter Eighteen

MAUDE

I shoved a pair of pink sweatpants and matching sweatshirt into my suitcase for our retreat weekend. Luckily, the bathing suit Piper helped me order had arrived in time. Spas meant hot tubs, pools, and those kinds of things. It'd been a couple of decades since I'd last donned a swimsuit. My old one had ended up in a pile for the thrift store years ago.

With a smile, I held up my new leopard print bikini. I'd only ever owned one pieces and thought, hell, why not? You only live once. If people didn't want to see my puckered prune-like skin, then they didn't have to look. If I'd had more time, I might've gotten some of that tanning lotion to darken me up some, too.

With a sigh, I went through the house, making sure I had everything I needed, then I shut off the lights and locked the doors. I wondered how far out of the city we were going. All Mr. Dancy would tell us was we'd be taking a bus somewhere.

Too bad he hadn't decided on a train or airplane. It would've been more comfortable and fun. But beggars couldn't be choosers. We were lucky he'd splurged for this bonding retreat, or whatever he wanted to call it. I half expected him to pull out laptops and make us work on new ideas next to a pool or something.

When I pulled into the parking lot, I spotted Piper standing with an olive green colored suitcase, her long auburn hair tied back in a ponytail. Kerrie waited beside her, holding a large maroon duffle bag that looked like it could've contained a dead body, it was so big.

Piper waved at me as I climbed from my car, tugging on the handle of my luggage to get it out of the backseat.

She hurried toward me. "Do you need help?"

"Nah, I've got it. Phew, this thing is heavy."

"Tell me about," Kerrie said, setting her bag on the ground. "I don't own any actual suitcases. And, of course, I didn't think to go buy one prior to today."

Across the lot, Wooyoung lingered next to a couple of young guys from the art and sales departments. He glanced at Piper, his eyes trailing over her, then caught me watching and quickly looked away. Hmm, did he still like her? If he did, why had he not tried to win her back?

I knew Piper had claimed he didn't want to be with her because she was hung up on her ex, but anyone with eyes could clearly see she had feelings for him, as well. But it wasn't my place to get involved this time. I'd given him the nudge to pursue her to begin with, now it was up to them. Although, maybe it wasn't a good idea for them to get together until Piper could let go of the past. *If* she could ever get over Minho. Either way, Wooyoung had done her wrong, too.

"Morning, chicas." Carlos approached us.

His luggage had tons of stickers and such on it like it'd been around the world a couple of times over. He looked dapper in his tight jeans and pullover sweater, although I thought he might roast in it. Now was not the time to be a fashionista.

"Morning," I said.

"Hey." Piper and Kerrie gave him a wave.

"I can't believe Mr. Cheap Pants is actually paying for us to all go somewhere." Carlos peered around the parking lot.

"Speaking of Mr. Cheap Pants, where in the world is he? He said to be here no later than six forty-five?" I searched for our boss, too. It wasn't like him to be late.

A loud horn playing what sounded like a rooster in heat blared as a large army green bus with trees painted and the words *Poshitively Urban* written on the side came barreling into the lot.

"Holy shit. Is that a school bus someone painted over?" Piper's mouth gaped as she took in the monstrous metal beast. "I thought I left these kinds of busses behind in high school."

"Why do I get the feeling this retreat is not going to be what we thought?" Kerrie caught my gaze, the look of fear radiating.

I laughed nervously. "It's not too late for us to make a run for it."

Mr. Dancy climbed off the bus wearing what I can only describe as an outfit you'd expect to see in Jurassic Park. He had on khaki shorts, which hung to his knees, almost touching the white socks he had pulled up past his calves with brown sandals adorning his feet. His tan button up shirt had a patch with trees on it sewn to the sleeve. Perhaps a remnant from some Boy Scout type troop he once belonged to and failed to advance beyond the first patch? Atop his head he wore a safari hat. At this point, I was sure he'd haul out a hunting rifle or treasure map.

"Ah, good, you're all here. Let's get lined up and on the bus. We have a busy day ahead of us." He grinned, flagging us forward.

"When in Rome," Piper said, rolling her suitcase up to the bus.

Mr. Dancy handed her a slip of paper. What had he given her? A moment later, I found out for myself. A coupon for half off the Poshitively Urban stay.

"Make sure to hang onto your coupons, everyone. We're being given a discount for being their first clients." He clapped his hands together like this was a good thing.

"Jesus H. Christ," I muttered. "He's gone and lost his mind."

"Also, I think Piper was right, this is definitely an old school bus." Kerrie ran her hand over one of the poop brown pleather seats.

"I thought I'd hit rock bottom when my boyfriend left, but nope. This is taking over the top spot on my list." Carlos snorted, following us toward the back of the bus.

"Two people to a seat everyone," Mr. Dancy said as if we were in elementary school and he was the principal.

"I'll admit, I'm quite terrified to find out where we're going," I whispered as I slid into a seat, followed by Carlos. Piper and Kerrie sat across the aisle from us, both wearing the same mystified expression that was on our whole company's faces.

"Same. I wouldn't put it past him to drop us off at some boot camp or something." Carlos cringed as if realizing his nightmare might come to fruition.

"Don't speak it into words," Piper chastised. "Think only positive thoughts."

"You mean, *poshitive* thoughts?" Kerrie laughed.

Piper nudged her with her leg. "Ugh, this is no joking matter. This is probably some weird thing Mr. Dancy did to get back at us for having our fans on at the office."

"Let's not panic just yet. Who knows, maybe he'll surprise us," I said, crossing myself.

But like the others, I knew Mr. Dancy well enough to be worried.

"Now, before we pull out, I need everyone to take one of the waiver papers I'm handing out, as well as a pen. Once they're all turned in, we'll be off."

When Mr. Dancy got to us, I glanced at the form he gave me. "What kind of waiver is this?"

"Oh, it's just something stating we won't hold retreat owners liable for any injuries or such during our trip." He waved it off like it was nothing. "It's just a release, Maude."

"It says something here about maiming or drowning? Where in the hell are we going?" Piper peered at me over the top of her waiver form.

"You got me, kid." I shrugged, and likely against my better judgment, I signed it. "So much for a spa weekend, I guess."

"Spa?" Mr. Dancy laughed. "No, spa. Think more adventure camp and bonding."

And with those final words, the bus jerked as it drove out of the lot and onto the main road. We wound around the city until we came to the outskirts of town. Suddenly, the bus lurched, then sped up to a gate with razor wire looped over the top, kind of like in prison movies. Sweet Jesus, had he brought us to a prison?

Next to me, Carlos cursed under his breath. "Now, I'm fearful. We have time to say a prayer, girls. We might need divine intervention."

"Um, we could hop out the emergency exit," Piper suggested. "But it might be a painful fall to the cement if we're moving."

The gate door slid open, and we entered the oversized parking lot. In the distance, I noticed a huge factory type building. And this was where the bus came to a stop. The brakes hissed, and the door swung open.

"Okay, everyone, get your coupons out, and we'll head inside." Mr. Dancy reached to grab a backpack from the floor under his seat.

I trudged into the aisle. "So much for our spa weekend."

I'm not sure what I thought we'd encounter when we walked in the door, but it wasn't what I got. A gasp escaped my lips as I searched the room. There were TV monitors mounted to the walls with a woodland scene playing while the sound of water trickling came from hidden speakers. There were faux trees made of metal while fake plants stood in pots. Even the ceiling had monitors hooked to it, showing pictures of a blue sky and clouds rolling by.

"What in the actual hell?" Piper whispered, looping her arm through mine.

"Hello, everyone, and welcome to Poshitively Urban. I'm Karolina with a 'K,' and I'll be your tour guide through the mystical places inside. You'll find tropical paradises, beaches, woods, rivers, and lakes. And maybe even a few animal surprises along the way." Her blonde curls bounced like tiny springs.

"Did she say animals?" I asked Kerrie, who'd set her bag at our feet.

"Yeah, but are they real or metal like the foliage?"

"Real. Holy shit!" Piper jumped back. "There's a snake!" She practically leapt into Carlos's arms to get out of the way as the reptile slithered across the floor at our feet.

Its long brownish gray base was peppered with reddish-brown stripes or squares. It looked like a familiar breed, maybe a boa? But the question remained, was it venomous?

"Oh, Frank the Snake won't hurt you. He's more scared of you than you are of him." Karolina with a K smiled. Her green eyes were glazed over.

Was she high?

"I don't do snakes," Piper said.

Karolina picked up the snake and let it wind around her arm. I had no idea what kind it was, but I was in the same boat as Piper. I didn't like them.

"Anyone want to pet him?" Our guide held him up.

As a group, we collectively took a step back like we were trying to avoid Godzilla rather than a snake.

"There's a reason I'm a city girl." Kerrie picked her bag up off the floor again. Her gaze seemed to search for more animals. "Hopefully, nothing crawls or climbs into our bags and stuff."

"Alright, Frank, let's get you back into the main room."

Once Karolina had released the serpent to God only knew where, she led us into another room—a more open, spacious one. There were more faux metal trees, along with tents placed in different areas. Each one had a metal barrel type trash can with a fire burning inside. There were more monitors with scenes of forests and paths and such.

"Is that a river?" Carlos, eyes widened, pointing ahead of us.

I let out a low whistle. "I'll be damned, it sure looks like it."

There, at the center, was a winding lazy river, something you might see at a waterpark. There were even some rapids forming in it. On the bank of the simulated river, were some inner tubes, rafts, and even small canoes.

"This is one of our camping areas. You've each been assigned a group that you'll do activities and stay in a specific area overnight with. We have an island room with a beach, a tropical jungle, and so much more. There will also be mixers to allow for you all interact at once. Oh, and I can't forget to mention, we have climbing walls and trust bridges."

"What's a trust bridge?" One of the accountants raised their hand.

"It's a rope bridge you'll help one another over. You have to trust your coworkers and friends to get you across. It's a great team building exercise." She gestured to ropes hanging far above the river below.

"I don't think my old hips can take it," I said, for once happy to use my age as an excuse to get out of something.

"We have plenty of safety gear. You'll do just fine." Karolina had an overabundance of happiness and encouragement to give.

And it was annoying.

"Obviously, we can't force you to do this, but we highly recommend everyone at least make the attempt *if* you can. It really is a great morale building experience," Karolina added, I assumed for my benefit.

"I think I need a drink," Kerrie said. "Why in the heck didn't we grab a bottle of something strong before we got on the bus?"

"Yeah, where's the tiki bar?" Carlos grinned.

Karolina laughed her tinkly bright laugh. "Sorry, no alcohol allowed. You'll have a great retreat everyone. Now, I have the group lists right here that Mr. Dancy provided me."

"Jesus, we're doomed," I muttered. There were moments in life I looked back on and regretted, and I could tell me not missing the bus this morning, would be one of them.

"Remember, everyone, this is to help us be better workers," Mr. Dancy said, mirroring Karolina's positivity. I'm not sure if I imagined it or not, but his gaze seemed to linger on my group.

"Your first challenge? To find your tents and get your beds set up for the night. Each tent will need to be pitched. Then, you'll get your cots assembled. Now, let's read off our groups. Wooyoung, Carlos, and Edmund, you're in tent one, which is in the island area. You'll have to hike through the woods to get there." She gestured to a door to our left, fake ivy and foliage hanging from the ceiling. "Group two, Piper, Maude, and Kerrie, you'll be in tent two. You will need to make your way through the jungle. Watch out for sudden rainstorms and friendly critters." She touched my arm, prompting us toward a door straight ahead of us, following the river, which seemed to go beneath the wall.

She continued to read off names until everyone had a designated spot. "At each site, you'll find supplies such as food, water, items to make a fire, as well as a tablet. The tablet will need to be logged into, and you'll find three activities you'll be required to complete with your group. When you're done with those, you'll be teamed up with another group for a bigger challenge tomorrow. If there are no questions, go ahead and be on your way."

"If I'd have known we'd have to go hiking, I'd have brought Sophie's backpack instead of this duffle." Kerrie attempted to situate it on her shoulder, but to no avail.

"Maybe we can make it like a backpack. Here, let's try to get the handles around both your shoulders." Piper set her suitcase down and went to help Kerrie. A few minutes later, they managed to rig it enough to keep from slipping.

"Shall we head out then?" I asked, wondering what in the world Mr. Dancy had gotten us into.

"Yeah, I can lead if you guys want." Piper clutched a small map that Karolina had handed her.

"Do you even know how to read that thing?" My gaze shifted over the piece of paper she held. Damn, the writing was tiny.

"Mostly. Besides, how hard can it be? We're in a building."

Kerrie patted her arm. "Never tempt fate. If we're too optimistic, something bad will surely happen."

Not that I was superstitious, but I happened to agree with her on this one.

With Piper in the lead, we pushed through a heavy metal door. Instantly, the air became hotter and more humid. The amount of metal trees and potted plants multiplied tenfold. There were ferns and vines growing everywhere. Were these ones real? I squinted and tried to determine if they were. There was also dirt beneath our feet, too.

The sounds of birds and monkeys echoed around us. From the river, spurts of water flew as an alligator or crocodile lunged, snapping its teeth at us as if prepared to drag us underwater and end our misery.

"Ugh, fuck!" Piper jumped back, nearly knocking Kerrie and I over.

"Wait, that thing is animatronic, it's not real." Kerrie still held her hand to her chest, her face paler than it had been when we'd entered.

My heart beat rapidly in my chest, sweat pooling under my boobs. "Judas, how is this anything like a spa weekend?"

Piper laughed. "Sorry, I'm so freaking jumpy now. I mean, first the snake, which I may remind you all is real and roaming around, and now this movie set creature."

My eyes shifted to the trees above, searching for more real snakes. "How realistic do you guys think they made the jungle?"

"Jury is still out on that." Kerrie continued forward, following after Piper who'd finally started moving again.

We hadn't gotten very far when a rumble of thunder sounded and rain fell, drenching us.

"Do you think Mr. Dancy had us get assigned to the jungle on purpose?" Kerrie reached out to keep me from slipping in the mud.

"Oh, I wouldn't put it past that man." I wiped my wet hair from my face. So much for styling it earlier. Instead of sitting around, enjoying drinks with tiny umbrellas, I was trying to survive a monsoon.

A low roar echoed around us, and we went still once more.

"That sounded like a big cat." Piper shot me a desperate look. "What kinds of cats live in jungles?"

"Um, I don't know. Panthers and jaguars, maybe. Why? Do you think they let some loose in here?" Kerrie squeezed in close to us. "Did any of you bring a weapon?"

"Nope, fresh out of rifles and machetes. Didn't think we'd need them this trip." I tried to stay calm, but my pulse soared. If I got out of this place without having a heart attack, it'd be a miracle.

"Let's keep moving. I'm scared something will get us if we stop. Like we'll be more of a target." Piper reached for my arm, pulling me along. Her suitcase almost tipped over as she dragged it through the mud, but she didn't slow.

"According to the map, our camp should be at a bend in the river," Piper said, although she no longer held the map.

I hoped she remembered it correctly. Last thing I wanted to do was get lost in the faux jungle with who knew what skulking about.

"How long have we been walking? It feels like hours." I wiped more sweat from my brow. I hadn't sweat this much since I did that Richard Simmons aerobics tape back in the eighties.

"Twenty-five minutes," Kerrie said, looking at her watch. "How the hell could we have been traveling for that long? The building didn't appear that big when we pulled in, did it?"

"I honestly don't even know how to answer that. But our making bad time is probably because the trail is muddy, and the foliage, although most of it is fake, is thick." I swatted at a mosquito. Great, another thing to be on the lookout for. "Did anyone bring bug spray?" We were beginning to sound like broken records every time one of us asked if someone had brought something. We obviously weren't prepared for this trip.

"Nope, another thing left off my packing list." Piper turned and sneered at us. "Remind me to smack Mr. Dancy the next time he brings up a great bonding trip idea."

"Oh, you won't need a reminder. In fact, I'll likely beat you to it," I said.

At last, we came to a clearing on the bank of the river. Here, we found a large zipped case which held our tent. Along with the case was a barrel for our fire, three cots that we'd have to put together, a cooler, and a raft tied off on the shore.

We dropped our luggage, stretching our arms and backs.

"Okay, let's get this stupid thing set up." Piper tugged the tent from its bag and proceeded to spread it out. She also found stakes, poles, and rope inside, along with a mallet.

"Are there any directions?" I asked, staring at the bright orange material that would act as our home for the next two nights.

"No, but I think we put the poles together and slide them through these slots in the sides of the tent." Piper showed us.

So, the three of us went to work trying to weave poles into thin strips of fabric, cursing each time one got stuck. Once we got that part done, we found stakes which we got put into the ground or floor or whatever the heck we were standing on.

"Let's get our cots inside in case it rains again," I said.

We fumbled to get the three cots lined up. They barely fit, but at last we had them arranged. To my surprise, it wasn't so bad inside. We could unzip the windows so we could stare out the screens and let in some air.

"Do you think anything will crawl in here with us?" Kerrie peered around, setting her bag on top of her bed.

"I sure as heck hope not," I muttered, opting to put my suitcase on my cot, too, at least until we could scout out the area. "Did anyone see the tablet we're supposed to log into?"

"Yeah, it was by the fire can thing. I can go grab it really quick," Piper offered.

She came back with the book-sized black device. Piper logged into it with the password that'd been written on our map. "Alright, so it looks like we have three challenges. Our first is to raft the rapids. Once we're done with that, we have to figure out how to start our fire and cook a meal together. And the last one says we'll have to wait to get the final challenge until we've completed the first two."

I groaned. "I don't like the sound of that."

"We should change into our swimsuits if we're going to be rafting. No sense getting all our clothes wet." Kerrie shoved her hair back from her face and opened her bag to rummage through. She pulled out a black one piece bathing suit and pair of flip flops.

Piper and I quickly did the same, grabbing our swim garments, as well. Once done, I adjusted my leopard-print bikini, making sure nothing was hanging out where it shouldn't be.

"Looks like I picked the right print to fit into the jungle," I said with a smile.

Kerrie laughed. "Yeah, well, let's hope we don't meet up with any real leopards."

When we were all changed, we made our way out of the tent and toward the raft. Inside, we found three life jackets and three paddles.

I stared out across the river. It was approximately twenty to twenty-five feet from our side of the shore to the other, if I had to guess. The brown water reminded me of our local rivers, and I wondered if they pumped the water in from one of them. Wherever it came from, it was definitely real. Kind of like an amusement park lazy river, but flowing faster. Nothing in this room area was reminiscent of being in a building. There was no spot where you could see the walls. Everything was covered in real or faux greenery and plants. Vegetation was so thick in some places, you could see but a few feet in front of you. Save for the ceiling, which did have some built-in monitors that showed the changing sky. But had someone not pointed out that they were digital screens, I might never have guessed, it was that realistic.

There were even elevation changes throughout, along with mud, dirt, rocks, vines, not to mention the humid temperature. It honestly made me think of the documentaries I'd watched about the Amazon. The whole area we were in gave off jungle vibes.

"Anyone ever been rafting before?" I asked.

Piper nodded. "Once with my stepdad when we took a trip out west. But I was like thirteen or fourteen at the time."

"I've never been on a boat before." Kerrie frowned.

"Wait, does everyone know how to swim?" I stared at the girls, who both nodded yes. "Thank goodness. At least we won't drown, or I hope we won't. Maybe they'll have some Tarzan-type lifeguards along the river."

"Funny!" Piper snorted. "I think we're on our own for this. Maude, do you think you'll be okay doing this?"

With a chuckle, I nodded. "I'm older, but I'm not as frail as I seem. I do work out, you know."

Kerrie and I climbed into the raft first, while Piper undid the rope and shoved us off the bank. She quickly hopped in, nearly sending us flying over the edge.

"Okay, everyone grab a paddle. To go straight, we need to paddle on both sides. If we want to turn the raft, we only paddle on one side. Let me show you."

Piper demonstrated what to do, and we followed her lead. For a moment, I felt myself relax as we drifted down the river. This wasn't so bad, or so I thought. I watched the scenery as we floated by. It was kind of pretty in a fake, Wizard of Oz Munchkin Land way.

"Does it sound like the water is getting louder?" Kerrie asked, interrupting my reverie.

Piper's brow furrowed, her eyes widening. "You've got to be kidding me."

"What?" My fingers gripped tighter to my paddle. I peered around, not sure what I was searching for.

"There are actual rapids ahead. As in, things are about to get rough, ladies. Try to keep us straight and watch out for rocks," she said.

"Rocks? Are they trying to kill us? We're not professional whitewater rafters," I said.

"Apparently, it's okay to kill people if you're trying to help them bond and they signed release forms," Kerrie said.

"Yeah, we'll bond in death." Piper shook her head as water splashed her face. "Okay, ladies, paddle when I tell you to, and try to stay in the boat."

She hollered out commands, letting me and Kerrie know when to paddle. We raced forward like we were on an amusement park ride. The raft dipped low, sending waves up over us. I sputtered, thankful for my life preserver. We battled the rapids for what seemed like hours when I knew only minutes had gone by. My arms were like rubber, and I wasn't sure how much more paddling I'd be able to do.

The roar of the water got louder, and Piper swore.

"What now?" I turned to look at her.

"Waterfall," she said. "Take a deep breath, we're going over."

Sucking in air greedily, I didn't have time to brace myself. The next thing I knew, we were going ass over tea kettle down a small waterfall. Time stopped as we flew from the raft. Water rushed over my head, and I kicked my legs, propelling myself to the foamy surface. I made my way toward the shore. Next to me, I noticed Piper and Kerrie doing the same.

"Jesus H. Christ. If Mr. Dancy wanted me to retire, he just had to ask, no need in trying to kill me off. I'm in good shape for my age, but hot damn!" I climbed to the shore, trying to catch my breath and adjust my breast snuggly back into my top. My seventy plus year old body was not in the same shape it used to be. I should be playing shuffleboard in a retirement community, not plunging over waterfalls.

Kerrie laughed. "Well, are we bonded now?"

"I think we were bonded before this unnecessary trip." Piper stood, wringing water from her hair. "I'd say we should salvage the raft, but I'm not swimming downstream to catch it."

"Me, either," I said. "I'm way too old for this horse cocky!"

"Ugh, you realize we have to climb back up there to get to our camp?" Kerrie placed her hands on her hips, glowering at the rock wall in front of us.

"Can we just lay rocks out in an SOS pattern and be rescued?" Or maybe there was an elevator somewhere.

However, upon further inspection, I found nothing to help us. No flares, or phones, or Coast Guard. Nothing.

"Wait, here's some rope on the shore. I think it was supposed to be for tying the raft off, but since we no longer have a raft, we can use it for climbing. Let me go up first, then I can tie it off up there and help pull you guys up." Piper tossed her life jacket onto the ground.

Piper climbed quicker than I thought she would. Soon, she tossed the rope down to us. Kerrie climbed up next, struggling to get a good grip. But at last, she heaved herself up and over as well.

Now, it was my turn, but before I started to make the attempt, Piper groaned then hollered down to me. "Wish I would've seen those sooner." She pointed to the side off the faux rocks where partially hidden stairs had been carved into the wall of rock. "Well, I guess I got a full workout today."

"Lucky for me." I heaved a sigh of relief. At least, I wouldn't chance falling off the rope and breaking my hip. Taking the stairs, I met up with the girls.

When we reached the top of the rock wall, we trudged in the direction of our camp. Never did I think I'd be so excited to see a tent in my life. We changed, then Piper went over to the barrel trying to figure out how to get a fire going.

"Wait a second, you guys. I think this is actually a propane grill or stove made to look like a can." She gestured to the knobs on the side of it.

"I think you're right." I stood behind her and peered over her shoulder.

While Piper messed with the knobs on it, Kerrie and I found a sack with various food items tucked behind our tent. Someone had likely placed it there after we'd left on our rafting trip.

Damn people probably videotaped the whole escapade.

"Grill is now going," Piper said. "Who knew camping trips and grilling with my stepdad would prove to be detrimental to our spa weekend survival."

We made hotdogs over the flame and found snack-sized bags of chips and cans of beans to go with it.

"I'm normally not a hotdog person, but this tastes good."

"It might've been our brush with death that made you hungry enough to devour them." Kerrie grinned.

"So, what's next on our challenges? Or dare I ask?" I wiped my hands on a napkin, then threw it in the fire.

Piper grabbed the tablet. "Challenge three is, in your group, come up with the perfect greeting card idea."

"You're kidding, right?" I snorted. "Of course, leave it to Mr. Dancy to get some work out of us through all this. Can't say we didn't see this coming."

Kerrie cleared her throat. "Or we can skip the card stuff and maybe talk about other things." Her voice got softer as if there was something she wanted to say to us, but wasn't quite sure how start.

"Like what?" Piper set her half-eaten bag of chips on the ground next to her.

"I don't know, possibly tell one another a secret we haven't told anyone else?" Kerrie glanced between us.

"I-I'm game if you guys are." Piper rubbed her hands against her leg. "There's something I kind of want to get off my chest."

We all got quiet. I swallowed hard. There was only one secret I was harboring, but was I ready to share it yet? As I watched the girls, I realized they were the closest I had to family now.

Piper fidgeted with a string on her shirt, then began. "I-I can go first. I'm a chicken, in the sense that I don't want to turn out like my mom, who has been married so many times. I thought because of my relationship with Minho, there's no way I'd be like her. But then he cheated and left. I've had a super hard time letting him go." Tears welled in her eyes. "The truth is, Wooyoung breaking up with me is kind of my fault. I never truly gave him a chance."

"He still shouldn't have kept secrets," Kerrie said.

"She's right, he shouldn't have. But you also need to learn to let go, Piper. You have so much to offer the right man." I gave her hand a squeeze.

"I really screwed up with Wooyoung, and the sad part is, I think I've fallen in love with him. That's my secret. That I love him, but don't know how to tell him or show him. I mean, my mom was never the huggy-lovey, show-your-kid-affection kind of parent."

We moved to hug her. "After our trip, you have to tell him."

Kerrie nodded. "She's right. You have to at least try."

"Alright, my confession is over. Someone else's turn." Piper wiped her eyes with the back of her hand.

Kerrie wrung her hands together. "I'll go now. I know I've implied Hal and I are on good terms with our divorce, but the truth is, we're not. I'm only living there because I can't afford a place of my own. He literally brings other women into our house and has sex in *our* bed with them. And he expects me to cook, clean, do all the running for the kids, and all the while he's off having a good time. When he asked for a divorce, he told me I wasn't fun anymore." This time, she teared up, watching for our reactions. "He made me promise not to tell the kids or his family about our divorce because he didn't want to be the bad guy."

"He *what*?" Piper screeched. "That selfish bastard is the bad guy. What an asshole!"

Kerrie laughed and cried simultaneously. "I know. I've been so weak in all this, worried if I said or did the wrong thing, he'd kick me out. But I'm done lying for his sake."

"Good girl. You're stronger than you think," I said.

"I'm trying."

Piper rubbed her shoulder. "This is why we have the no penises allowed club."

"Well, except for Carlos," I added.

They giggled. "What about you, Maude?" Piper turned to me.

I swallowed past the lump in my throat, trying to form words. In the end, I just blurted it out for the sake of getting it over with. "Corny didn't really leave me. I mean, he *left* me, but not in the same sense as your beaus did. Corny passed away."

Both women gasped, then were silent for several seconds before Piper moved closer. "Maude, oh God. Why didn't you say something?"

She embraced me, then was joined by Kerrie. They held me while I cried. Tears I'd been holding in for so long. My chest tightened as I recalled the phone messages, the trip to the hospital, the words the doctor uttered. *He's gone.* A lump formed in my throat, my sinuses burning.

"Corny lied to me. He was supposed to be taking his medication for various health conditions and hadn't been doing it. For months, he didn't even refill his prescriptions. Corny died from a ruptured brain aneurysm. Something that *could've* possibly been prevented. I'm just so damned angry with him. Fifty years of marriage, and he didn't even tell me he'd quit taking his meds. If I'd paid closer attention or he'd shared this with me, I could've fought to make sure he'd kept up on his health. I could've taken care of him. I-I wouldn't have let him exhaust himself driving me to and from work." I hiccupped through more tears. "I'm not sure whether to be sad, or mad, or what."

"There's no right way to grieve," Piper said. "When my dad passed, I was numb for the first bit, then I had a stage of acting out and crying. But I wish you would've told us sooner. We could've done more for you."

Emptiness seemed to swallow me. My body sagged against my friends, their arms the only thing keeping me upright as the dam finally broke. "Not much anyone can do. He's gone. Corny's gone, and he's never coming back." I sobbed, letting the grief finally overtake me. "Somedays, I feel as if I might perish from a broken heart. I mean, how do I keep going on without him?"

"We'll be here, Maude. We're not going anywhere," Kerrie said. "We'll get through all this together."

"Agreed, we have one another." Piper clutched us tighter. "From now on, no more secrets between us."

Like angels, Kerrie and Piper consoled me. Maybe Mr. Dancy had been right. Maybe we had needed this bonding weekend in the metal jungle.

Chapter Nineteen

PIPER

A loud horn blared the next morning, rousing me from sleep. I let out a groan, my back aching from a night spent on a cot.

"Make the sound go away," Kerrie murmured, covering her head with a pillow.

"Not likely in this place." Maude snorted, pulling herself up into a sitting position.

"Alright, campers, time to get up, have breakfast, and make your way to the main camping area," Karolina's annoying voice came over the loudspeakers.

How could she be this chipper this early? Maybe she'd partaken in a little of nature's weed or something.

"It isn't realistic to have Karolina waking us up on a retreat. In a jungle, it should be the sounds of nature or rain." I gave a yawn. "So much for realism."

"And sleeping in," Kerrie added. "I never get to sleep in. I was actually excited to have this weekend to recuperate from all the running I've been doing."

Swinging my feet over the edge of my cot, I sat glancing at the other two, recalling our confessions last night. If there was one thing I realized, it was that I wasn't the only broken one. We were all broken in some way or another—and that brokenness had somehow brought us together.

I had no idea what today would bring, but I was ready for it. Even though I was tired, I felt sort of mentally refreshed. Finally, I kicked my blanket off and hurried to get dressed, wondering if we might be able to shower or if we'd have to bathe in the river later.

We got dressed, then went outside to find someone had added eggs, bacon, and bread to our cooler. I got the grill going again and grabbed a cast iron skillet to cook in. I fried up the bacon, dumping some of the left-over grease in an empty bean can from last night's dinner. The rest of the grease I used to keep the eggs from sticking to the bottom of the pan.

Maude grabbed the bread and used the pronged sticks to toast it over the flames. When it was done, we sat back and enjoyed our food. I cleaned up the pan with some water from the river and put it on top of the cooler.

After everything was taken care of, we grabbed our bags and suitcases, and made our way back through the makeshift jungle toward the main camping area.

Soon, we arrived to find our fellow staff members waiting in a large circle, Karolina at the center. God, what was she having them do now? It looked like some sort of warm-up exercise. Or perhaps they were meditating? It was hard to tell from here.

"Yay, everyone is here now. Ladies, please stretch out for our next task." Karolina's smile nearly maimed my eyes with its brightness.

Carlos gestured for us to join him. "Phew, I was worried you guys didn't survive." He eyed Maude, who donned a pair of shorts with a red and white halter top. "Dang, Maude, if I was twenty years older, and not gay, I'd totally date you."

She snorted and waved him off. "I'm no cougar. I like my men older."

"Sorry to hear that." He grinned, giving her a wink. "So, what was your camping area like?"

"You mean our death trap?" I quirked an eyebrow. "Seriously, we had to traverse the jungle, which was hotter than Satan's ass crack, we almost died twice, once by animatronic alligator jaws, and a second time by going over a waterfall in a raft."

His nose wrinkled, mouth turned down in a frown. "Are you serious?"

"She's dead serious," Kerrie said. "It was complete madness."

"Honey, you don't know madness until you had to boat out to an island."

I chuckled. "An island?"

"Yeah, don't ask me how in the hell they managed to make an island, but this place was surrounded by water. It had a few trees on it, but was mostly sand. Partway through setting up our tents, a huge storm blew in. The waves were crashing so badly, we couldn't leave. We had to forage for food that washed up on shore. I was having a real Tom Hanks in *Cast Away* moment, only without Wilson the ball."

"You had Edmund and Wooyoung," I said.

He smirked. "Yes, I did get to look at those fine men all night. However, when facing imminent death, you kind of lose the enjoyment of the moment."

"True." Maude nodded. "But see here, we're all back together again."

"Right, only problem being, I feel like we're about to be tortured again," I said.

Sure enough, once Karolina made sure we were all stretched out, she clapped her hands together. "Everyone, can I have your attention please? Today we are going to work together as a whole group. I mentioned the trust bridge when you got here, and now, we're going to make it a reality. I have some gear for you all to put on, then we'll make our way up. Your goal is to cross the rope bridge over to the mountain." She pointed to a large rocky-looking area constructed of metal, cement, and faux trees.

I swallowed hard, wrenching my hands together. The only thing I hated more than snakes was heights. No way could I do this. It was so far above the river. And if I fell, was the water deep enough to keep me from dying? Or would the impact of the fall kill me first?

"You okay?" Kerrie touched my arm. "You're super pale."

"I, um, sorta hate high places." Which was the understatement of the century. A few other people came to help Karolina get us harnessed in. At least they were using safety precautions, which meant there wasn't much chance of injury.

My stomach churned as a wave of nausea washed over me.

Karolina had people line up and start making their way up the to the rope bridge above. However, I lingered where I was, letting everyone else cut in front of me. My hands fisted at my sides as I watched each person take steps across the unstable ropes.

From above, Maude cursed. Carlos cheered her on, and at last, she made it.

Soon, I was the only one left to go. Taking a deep breath, I forced my wobbly legs forward and began to climb. Sweat beaded my brow. When I got to the top, I clung tight to the sides of the bridge. The word 'bridge' was a very loose definition for this rope monstrosity.

Suddenly, my feet no longer wanted to move. Mouth dry, I attempted to suck in deep breaths of air.

"I can't do this," I said. No sense in pretending otherwise.

"No one's going to force you." Karolina gave me one of her annoying smiles. "You can just say the words and quit now. We'll help you back down."

Annoyed, I glowered at her. Was she seriously calling me a quitter?

"Come on, Piper, you've got this," Kerrie shouted.

"Piper, don't you dare turn back. Come to us," Maude said. "Us girls stick together, so get a move on. You climbed the rock wall yesterday and navigated the rapids. This is nothing compared to those things. Grab the bull by the balls."

"I think you mean horns," Carlos shouted.

"No, I mean balls."

I took a hesitant step, but when the bridge started to swing again, I stopped. My lids squeezed shut. I stood there until I felt the sway of the rope from someone else moving. I opened my eyes to find Wooyoung making his way toward me.

"Piper, don't look down, okay? Look at me." He reached me, clutching my hand in his. "I want you to hold onto my waist. I'll help you get to the other side. All you have to do is keep staring straight ahead and put one foot in front of the other."

"I'm scared," I whispered.

"I know, but you can do this. Do you trust me?"

His mahogany gaze swept over me, cocooning me in warmth. Did I trust him? I mean, he'd lied to me about his sister, however, I never believed for one moment he'd intentionally let harm come to me.

"I...yes, I do."

"Then come with me," he said softly.

Heart thudding like a charging rhino, I gripped onto Wooyoung's waist, and he led me over the bridge. Several times I wanted to give up, yet I didn't.

Wooyoung's back and shoulder muscles were taut as we made it to the other side. Once there, I released him, and everyone cheered.

"Thank you," I said to him.

He nodded, then rejoined his friends. And just like that, he was back to ignoring me. Before I could become too emotional about it, Maude and Kerrie hugged me.

"I knew you could do it." Kerrie patted my back.

"Me, too," Maude said. "Although, having a well-built Wooyoung leading the way didn't hurt, am I right?"

My cheeks burned. "I have no idea what you're talking about."

"Sure, sure." Maude grinned.

Karolina led us down a steep trail to the other side of the river where there were grills set up cooking various food items. There was even wine. So much for the no alcohol rule.

"I thought you said no alcohol?" Carlos said, handing his climbing harness to one of the workers.

"That was before the challenges. We didn't want anyone intoxicated during their foray into the wilderness." Karolina handed out several glasses. "But this is to celebrate all you've achieved here."

"Wait, are we done with all our bonding activities?" I asked, running a hand through my loose hair. I'd lost my hair tie sometime after we'd gone over the waterfall yesterday.

"Not exactly. There are a couple of other small things, but nothing you can't have a drink before doing."

"Cheers," Kerrie said, accepting a glass of red wine.

"Cheers," Maude and I answered.

It turned out the other activities we had were cooking a big meal together and some weird tug of war thing. As we sat, listening to the sounds of "nature" later that night, I found myself watching Wooyoung across the fire. His dark hair was stuck to his forehead due to the humidity, but he still looked hot.

I missed him. However, I had no idea how to win him back. Well, I did, but how the hell did I get over Minho, who I'd spent half my life with? In the end, I knew I had to let Minho go and move on. Not just because I wanted Wooyoung in my life, but it'd be healthier for me, too, if I could stop grieving my breakup and relearn how to trust someone again.

"Penny for your thoughts." Maude nudged me out of the Wooyoung-laced trance I was in.

"A penny, that's kind of cheap," Carlos said with a laugh. "How about a quarter? You can at least get a piece of bubblegum out of a machine with that."

I rolled my eyes. "Just trying to figure out how to finally get over Minho and move on."

"Hmm, and I think I know the object of your affection that could help with that." Carlos winked, nodding at Wooyoung.

I shook my head. "No, I think I've screwed up too badly for that."

"Remember, he was in the wrong, too, and I don't think that ship has fully sailed yet," Kerrie said. "Not that I'm an expert in the area of love, but the way Wooyoung came to your rescue today proves he's not as over you as he pretends to be."

"He's a bad actor, too. He's not even good at pretending. You know how many times I've caught him watching you on this trip?" Maude held her fingers up and started counting. "Well, it's more times than I have fingers, I can tell you that."

"What I need is a plan, or to talk to someone who knows how to let people go." Who did I know like that? Then, it hit me. My mom. She was the expert at breaking up, leaving, divorcing, remarrying. Surely, she'd have some advice for me.

After the bus dropped us off in our work parking lot, I hurried home, not even accepting a ride from anyone who offered. It gave me time to think and mull over what I needed to do. Seeing my apartment for the first time in a few days, I felt relief flood through me. First thing I planned on doing was taking a shower, then I'd call Mom.

I had no idea if she was even in the States at this point. Last I'd been aware, she'd taken a trip out of country with her newest husband.

When I finished scrubbing the remnants of dirt and river water from my skin, I made my way back into the living room and sat on the couch, holding one of my throw pillows to my chest.

It was now or never. With a sigh, I picked up my cell phone and dialed her number. It rang twice before she picked up.

"Piper, hey what's wrong?" she asked, her voice crisp and melodic, just as I always remembered it to be.

"Does something have to be wrong for me to call?" My free hand gripped the arm of the chair, bracing myself for the lecture about my never calling her.

"Well, when else do you call?"

"Jesus, Mom, I called to talk for a few minutes. And besides, it's hard to know when you're available and not. Wasn't sure if husband six or seven took you on a trip or not."

"Husband seven has a name, you know," she said.

"Francois, I do know. I was teasing. If you're busy, I can call another time." Yep, I was a chicken when it came to confrontation with my mother.

"No, I'm not. Please don't hang up. It's been too long, Piper, since we actually had a conversation. I know you don't always agree with the things I do, but I still love you."

"I know." I took a deep breath. "The thing is, I need help. I want to move on from Minho, but don't know how. I met this really great guy, but he thinks I'm too hung up on mine and Minho's breakup to really be committed to him, and he's right."

"Well, you came to the right place," she said, somewhat sarcastically, but I caught the hint of seriousness behind her words, too. "I'm the expert on moving on and starting over."

I remained quiet, not arguing with her, because what she said was true.

"You need to give yourself closure," she said. "Whether that closure comes from you talking to Minho, moving to a different house, counseling, whatever your closure might be. I can't tell you what you need to do, I can only relay what's worked for me. But the biggest thing is to make a decision and see it through. If you're done with clinging to the idea of Minho, then be done with it. Wash him out of your life. He's not worth your tears. And admittedly, you're better without him, Piper. Find someone who will cherish you."

Tears welled in my eyes. "Thank you." For the first time in a long time, I felt close to my mom.

She'd hit the nail on the head. I was better off without Minho. I'd managed to live on my own without him. I was happier now having Maude and Kerrie, Carlos, and Wooyoung in my life. Although, Wooyoung was currently on hiatus from my social circle. I had a feeling I might be able to fix it. I just needed to brainstorm how.

"When I lost your father, it was excruciatingly painful," Mom said softly. "But your father made me promise to not waste my life in sorrow. He wanted me to be happy. So, his words became my closure. I know you think it was easy for me to move on, but it wasn't. However, I had you to think about, too, not just myself. I wanted to find someone who could fill the role of a father for you as well as be a companion for me." A sigh sounded on the other end. "And well, you know how that went. I met David. While he was someone who let me lean on him and helped me raise you, I realized it wasn't the kind of true love I'd had with your father. David was a true friend, one who did so much for us. Anyway, enough about me."

"Thank you," I said again, appreciating her honesty. Mom and I didn't normally do these kinds of serious talks, and I wasn't quite sure what to say at this point. This was the only time I'd ever heard her be so candid about my dad.

"You're welcome, sweetheart. Maybe when I'm in town next, we can meet up for dinner or a spa day."

I laughed. "I'm not sure I'm up for any spas anytime soon, but dinner would be great."

"I hate to cut this short, but Francois and I are meeting up with his parents to take the boat out. I'll talk to you soon?"

"Yeah, I'll give you call and let you know how everything turns out."

When we hung up, I went out on my deck and sat. I watched the waves crest and fall on the shore across the street. Things were changing again, but this time, I was ready. Ready to let go and dive in.

After a half an hour of sitting outdoors, my cell rang, and I hopped up to grab it. "Piper, hey, it's David."

My stepdad always identified himself, even though he'd had the same number for as long as I could recall. "Hi, what's up?"

"So, I'm downstairs and thought I'd check in on you since I was in the neighborhood."

With a snort, I headed toward my buzzer. "You mean, Mom called and asked you to make sure I was fine?"

"That, too." He laughed.

"Sure, come on up. I buzzed you in."

A few minutes later, David knocked on my door and I let him in. He smelled of sandalwood, a scent I always associated with him since before his and Mom's divorce. His brown hair was speckled with gray now, a reminder he was getting older. He still wore a friendly smile and gave the best bear hugs.

"Piper, how's my girl doing?"

"Better. Believe it or not, Mom's pep talk kind of helped."

I ushered him over to the couch. "Your mom is not always bad. She's a loving person. Um, maybe a little too loving sometimes," he teased.

"I wish she would've stayed married to you."

"In the end, we weren't right for one another, but I gained a daughter out of it, so it wasn't all horrible."

"Did Mom tell you why I called?"

"Yeah, she did. So, I wanted to let you know I do have an apartment available in another building if you decide you want to move. I know it won't have the view of Lake Michigan, but it's in a nice area."

David was a businessman and owned several apartment buildings in Chicago as well as a hotel chain, and a fancy restaurant, too. He had no other children, other than me, and even though I wasn't blood related, he'd always treated me as such.

"I'll think about it. Would I be able to check it out?" Might as well leave no stone unturned at this point.

"Of course. I'll call the building manager and let him know you might drop by, that you're to have full access to it. If you decide you want it, just let him know, and I'll take care of everything."

"Thank you." Honestly, I had no idea how I'd gotten so lucky to have so many great people in my life recently. Maybe everything really would be okay.

Chapter Twenty

KERRIE

It was so nice to get home on Sunday after the weekend retreat. For once, it felt like a weight had been lifted from my shoulders, having been able to finally be honest about my situation.

According to Sophie, Hal never came home for the weekend. Instead, it was his parents who'd come to stay with the kids. My mother-in-law was not happy with Hal, and I was sure he'd get an earful soon if he hadn't already.

I picked up a blue crayon and shaded in the water of the picture the kids had picked for me to color in one of their coloring books. Tommy and Nella sat beside me at the counter, each absorbed in their own art projects. Sophie was vegging in the living room, trying to catch up on one of her K-Drama shows. It was a peacefulness I'd come to look forward to.

The side door to the kitchen flew open, and Hal stormed in, his face red, his jaw tight.

"What the hell did you do?" he asked, coming right over to the counter.

Tommy and Nella cringed away from him.

"What are you talking about?"

"You know damn well what I'm talking about. You told my parents about our divorce. Now, they're pissed at me."

Sophie came into the kitchen, her eyes wide. She looked like she might open her mouth, but I interjected before she could.

"Soph, take Tommy and Nella upstairs, okay?"

"Mom?"

"It'll be alright, just go."

As soon as they left the room, I turned on Hal. "I wouldn't have had to tell your parents about the divorce if you'd fucking picked up your phone. You haven't called once to make sure Tommy was okay. He was rushed to the hospital by ambulance. You were supposed to be here that night, but you were too busy boinking whatever flavor of the week you were on. So don't yell at me. I'm tired of lying and living like this. You don't give two shits about the kids. It's one thing to be done with me, but quite another to act like they don't exist."

"You promised not to say anything. That was the condition of you staying here. Now my family thinks I'm a no-good asshole." He moved closer, his face inches from mine.

My heart leapt into my throat, wondering if he might hit me. I took a step back, bumping into a stool. "Don't put this on me. You made the choice to cheat, then ask for the divorce. I tried going along with your plan, but I'm tired of it. When you can't even check your messages or be here for our kids, I have to draw the line. They didn't ask for any of this, and they're the ones who are suffering."

"Don't use them as an excuse. You're just mad that I met someone else."

"Nope, guess again. That lady can have you and all your bullshit lies. You are a real piece of work, one who doesn't deserve the title of Dad."

"I want you out of this house tonight, do you understand? The divorce papers said I only had to let you stay for six months. I'm not dealing with your shit anymore." Hal slammed his fists on the counter.

Tears welled in my eyes. He wanted us out tonight? Where the heck were we going to go? The only reason I couldn't keep the house in the first place was because I couldn't afford the mortgage. So, the judge awarded it to him, with the clause I could stay in the marital home for six months while trying to save for my own place. Obviously, I should've lawyered up, too. I just never thought it'd come to this.

Just then, Sophie stepped into the kitchen, crying. "You're a jerk!" she shouted. "I hate you. I can't believe you're acting like this."

Hal glared at me. "See, you've even turned the kids against me."

"You did that yourself. For once, man up and take responsibility for your poor fucking choices." I moved to Sophie's side. "You want us gone, we'll be gone. I'm taking the kids' stuff when I go."

"Do what you got to do. I'll be back tomorrow, and you better be out of here."

When he left, Sophie turned to me and hugged me, sobbing against my shoulder.

"Shh, it'll be okay. I promise, I'll figure something out."

"Mom, I can get a job and help with bills. Whatever you need me to do."

"No, honey. It won't come to that. Go on up and start helping your brother and sister get things into bags or boxes, whatever you can find. I've got to make a few phone calls. When I'm finished, I can come up and help. I think we have empty bins in the garage or down in the basement. We can bring them up and start packing."

"Okay." She sniffled, wiping her eyes.

Once she left the room, I leaned against the counter, crying. What would we do? Oh, God. This was such a mess. But Hal was out of control, and I wanted nothing more than to punch his stupid face.

Reaching into my purse, I grabbed my cellphone. Who could I call? I scrolled through my contacts, and Maude's name jumped out at me. Fingers shaking, I pressed her contact information. The phone rang a few times before Maude's no-nonsense voice came on the other end.

"Hello, Kerrie? You didn't land in jail again, did you? Not sure I can bond you," she said with a chuckle.

I gave a weak laugh. "No, I, um, well…Hal got home, and he was angry at me for telling his parents about our divorce. We got into a huge fight. He's kicking me and the kids out of the house. We have until tomorrow to move everything."

"Jesus H. Christ. What a jerk. Where will you stay?"

A hiss of air left my lips. "I-I don't know yet."

"Well, I do. You and the kids can come stay with me. I've got plenty of room here. It's too big of a house for one old lady to live in by herself, you know."

"Maude, wait, you don't have to do that," I rushed. "I mean, I don't know what I can afford to pay you."

"Ah, those details can be hashed out later and, of course, I can do that. You said so yourself, you don't have anywhere else to go. I've got four bedrooms here. The girls can share one. There's a bed in there, so you'll have to grab an extra one. You and Tommy can both have your own rooms. They're already furnished, so just bring clothes or any toys and bedding you might need."

I wiped the wetness from my eyes. "Maude, I...thank you so much."

"That's what friends are for, Kerrie. I'll get ahold of Carlos to see if he can come help, and you call Piper. I'm sure she can drop in to help, too."

"Alright, thank you again. See you soon." When I hung up with Maude, relief flooded me. Thank God for putting her in our lives. Next, I dialed Piper's number, hoping she'd pick up.

It took her a couple of seconds, but soon she was on the line. "Hey, what's up?"

"Piper, sorry to bother you, but I wondered if you could come over to help me and the kids pack? Hal kicked us out. Maude said she could take us in, but we need more hands-on-deck and vehicles to transport stuff for the kids and I."

"Oh, my God! Are you guys okay?"

My throat thickened. "We will be, this just came on so sudden."

"Hold on a second." I heard her whispering to someone else and wondered who she had over. When she came back on, she said, "My stepdad, David, is here. He said we can swing by with his truck to grab any bigger items that might have to be moved."

"Piper, thank you! I seriously don't know what I'd do without you and Maude. I'll message you directions to the house. I'm such a wreck right now, I don't even know where to start."

"Don't worry, you have backup on the way. Hang tight, we'll see you soon."

She hung up with me, and I scrolled through my messages to see if Demarcus might be able to help, as well. Not that I wanted to bother him, but the more people we had, the quicker we could get things done.

He texted back that he had to work until seven, but would swing by after work to lend a hand. I thanked him, then went to grab boxes, bins, bags—anything I could find to pack things in.

Piper and David were first to arrive. She marched into the house, and the first thing she did was hug me. "I'm sorry this happened."

"Thanks. Just can't believe it's come to this."

"So, what do you need help with?" she asked, peering around the kitchen. "David and I can help with whatever you need."

Sophie came into the room carrying a box filled with toys and set it down, followed by my younger ones, each carrying a bag filled with clothes.

A knock sounded on the side door, and we all turned to find Maude and Carlos standing there. I waved them in.

"Chica, I'm sorry. Ugh, the words I'd say if there weren't kids around," Carlos said.

Sophie grinned. "You can cuss around us. Mom does all the time."

I flushed. "Not *all* the time."

"Uh, huh," Tommy inserted. "Remember when you said shit?"

"Tommy!"

Maude chuckled. "Well, there are worst things he could say, you know."

"Still, we don't say that word, it's naughty." I glowered at Carlos, who was doing a bad job at holding back a smile. "And don't encourage him."

"What do you need my help with?" Carlos took his jacket off, revealing his tanned biceps covered in tattoos beneath his dark shirt.

"Whoa, that's some cool ink." Sophie stepped closer to him to admire the work.

"Thanks. I designed some of them myself."

"Really?" Her brows rose in surprise.

"Carlos works in the art department at the greeting card shop," I said. "Hey, Sophie might want to talk to you some. She's pretty good at art herself."

"I mean, I dabble." Her cheeks reddened.

"While we're packing, you can show me some of your work." Carlos moved to follow her.

"Sophie's bed needs to be broken down, as we're taking that with us. The kids' clothes, toys, TVs, computers, that kind of stuff can be packed. I'll likely take half of the dishes, towels, blankets, and all our photos on the walls."

"Don't forget the puzzles, boardgames, and craft stuff, too," Sophie hollered from the other room.

"Right. Anything you kids want to go with us, pack it," I said. Our whole lives were now being packed away in a few bins and boxes. Things we'd bought or collected as a couple or a family. I ran my hand through my hair, tugging at it as I let out a hiss of air. My eyes welled. This was too much.

Tommy tugged on my shirt. "Mommy, will Daddy be mad at us forever?"

"Oh, sweetie. No. Of course not. He's not angry with you kids. He's mad at me."

"No. I think he's mad at all of us," he said.

"Hey, buddy, why don't you take me to your room and show me what you want packed. Got to make sure we get all the good things first," David said, catching my eye.

I mouthed the words *thank you* as they left the room.

Maude and Piper grabbed some bins and went to work. They'd hold up certain items from time to time, asking if I wanted them or not.

Damn, this sucked. This was our lives here. The kids had grown up in the house. I wanted everything, but knew I couldn't take it all.

A short while later, another knock sounded on the side door. This time, Demarcus stood outside. He'd changed out of his uniform, sporting jeans and a police department hoodie. I noticed he had Mya with him, as well.

I opened the door for them. "Hi, thank you guys for coming."

"No problem. How are you?" he asked.

"Hanging in there. Kind of in frantic packing mode at the moment."

He smiled at Maude and Piper. "Hello, ladies, so we meet again."

Maude snorted. "At least this time you're not having to put us in cuffs."

"Wait, what did you just say?" Sophie stared between us.

"Oh, well..."

"Your mom and Piper came to my rescue when a man got inappropriate with me. It kind of turned into a bar brawl and we got arrested," Maude said matter-of-factly.

"Whoa, whoa, whoa," David said, his mouth turning up at the corners. "You mean to tell me my daughter got arrested?"

Maude nodded. "Yep. We spent the night in the slammer."

"Mom?" Sophie stared at me again, then laughed, too. "Great, my mom has street cred now."

"Oh, dear Lord. Let's not blow this out of proportion." I tried to hide my face, as I reached for more plates to pack.

"Who'd have known I worked with a bunch of criminals." Carlos *tsked* at us. "Hold on, was that why you guys were late that day for work?"

"Yeah, Mr. Dancy was on us like a hound with a steak," Piper said.

"Don't tell your mother." David eyed Piper. "She'll insist we move you out of the city, for sure."

"I agree. Probably the less people who know, the better," I said.

Packing went quicker having more people, and I didn't have time to grieve or cry as there was too much to do.

"Before we leave, I feel like we should bust out all the windows or something," Piper said.

"Or leave rotten food in the registers and see if he finds it." Maude grinned. "Too bad his vehicle isn't here. We could key that on the way out, too."

"I'm going to pretend I didn't hear any of this." Demarcus shook his head, laughing. "Remind me to never make you ladies angry."

"A woman scorned should not be trifled with," Piper said.

Carlos joined us in the kitchen, holding up a painting Sophie had done of a medieval knight on horseback. "Kerrie, why didn't you tell me Sophie was so talented at art?"

"She's amazing, isn't she?"

"Yes. I was thinking, if you're alright with it, I could work with Sophie once a week. Maybe popover after work one night."

Sophie beamed. "I'd like that. Maude, do you have a place we'd be able to work on things?"

"The back screened in porch during the summer. In the winter, we might have to come up with some other arrangements." Maude patted Sophie's hand.

"Thank you, then yes, I'd like to do that." My daughter looked like she might cry again, only this time, happy tears.

Once everything was loaded into the vehicles, I took one last look at the house. We'd swiped half the food, half the dishes, the kids' things, and mine. Most importantly, I had the pictures of Sophie, Nella, and Tommy from birth until this year's school pictures. My throat thickened with emotion. I'd raised our babies here, and now, I had to say goodbye. However, I knew it was time for a new start.

My gaze flicked to where Tommy held David's hand, telling him about how he broke his arm, then I watched Nella cling to Maude and Piper. I realized they'd be okay. They still had me, and we had a new family now, one who would always have our backs. Maude, Piper, and all the others truly were a blessing.

It took us a bit to get across town, but when we pulled into Maude's driveway, Nella gasped.

"This is our new house? Mama, it has a yard. Maybe we can get a swing set."

"We'll have to wait and ask Maude, okay?"

"Okay."

When we all climbed out of the cars, the kids seemed so happy. "Wow, this place is huge," Sophie said. "I think it's bigger than our house."

"There's plenty of room for everyone. Now, you kids follow me. I'll show you to your new rooms. We'll have to pull out some more dining room chairs from the basement, but all in all, I think we'll do just fine." Maude held onto Nella's hand and led her to the stairs. "Sophie, you and Nella have the room at the end of the hall. You'll be able to see the backyard from the window seat there."

"Oh, my gosh, I love it." Sophie peered around the room, and immediately went to the window seat. "This will be perfect for reading or sketching."

"I think it'll be big enough for the two of you," Maude said to the girls. "We can have one bed on one side of the room, and the other bed on the opposite side. Both dressers can go between the beds. And there's a large closet. Feel free to decorate however you girls want."

"Thank you," I said to Maude. "This is so perfect for them."

"Maude, can I call you Grandma Maude?" Nella asked shyly.

"Of course, you can. I never had any grandchildren, so that'll be nice to be someone's grandma." She smiled, hugging Nella.

Maybe this truly was a blessing in disguise. We needed a place to go, and Maude didn't want to be alone. We could help one another.

"I figure the only things I'll ask you to pay for," Maude said as we headed back downstairs, "is any extra electricity and the food. Don't worry about rent or anything like that. The mortgage is paid off. We might need to get Wi-Fi for the kids, but that's doable."

"Maude, are you sure?" This was an extravagant gift.

"I'm very sure. You need to get on your feet. Besides, I don't mind having you all here. In fact, I look forward to having a full house again."

I hugged her. She'd never truly know how thankful I was.

David and Demarcus splurged for pizza, drinks, and chips. We sat around a campfire in the backyard eating. The kids were having a blast. Mya, Sophie, and Carlos were talking about art and K-pop groups. Tommy and Nella were playing with light sticks by the tree, and I sat visiting with everyone, taking in the night.

Demarcus stood. "We should probably head out now. I've got to be up early for work."

"I'll walk you to the car while Sophie and Mya say their goodbyes," I said.

We ambled down the driveway together.

"Are you sure you're okay?" he asked when we stopped next to his SUV.

"I will be. It's been a draining day."

Demarcus leaned down, clutching my face in his hands. "You're a strong woman, Kerrie, and a great mother. I know things seem kind of crazy now, but they'll settle down."

His lips brushed mine, sending shock waves through my whole body like a sonar. I pressed closer to him, allowing him to wrap his arms around me.

Someone cleared their throat, and Sophie said, "Should we come back?"

"I, um..."

"No, we're just finishing up our goodnights," Demarcus said.

I couldn't help but notice the excited look the girls shared before Mya climbed into Demarcus's vehicle.

My finger touched my mouth where his lips had just been. It was a new beginning. I had no idea where any of this would lead. A new house, a new man, a new chapter, all looming ahead of me.

Chapter Twenty-One

MAUDE

The scent of bacon sizzling in the pan made my mouth water. It'd been a while since I'd made a big breakfast like this. Kerrie stood by the griddle, making pancakes, while I manned the meat and eggs. She and the kids had already been here a week. It had taken me a hot minute to get used to all the noise of the younger two, but I found I actually loved it. When Corny had passed, it'd gotten too quiet in here, almost unbearably so.

I imagined if my son, Layton, had not died in the Gulf War at the early age of twenty, I might've had some of my own grandchildren running around, although they likely would've been closer to Sophie's age, or older by now.

Nella sat at the table, braiding her Barbie's hair, while Tommy played on the floor in the living room with some of his race cars. Kerrie had gotten him a small rug with roads and such printed on it for him to roll his toy cars and trucks on.

Rays of sunlight peeked through the curtains, and I smiled. I never thought I'd find happiness again after Corny died. It still hurt to think about him lying to me. Some nights, I laid awake crying, questioning why God took him from me. Others, I cursed his name into my pillow before falling into a restless sleep. The truth was, my heart still hurt. If Kerrie and her kids hadn't moved in, I'm not sure how I would've continued to deal with his loss. But I still struggled in the quiet moments before everyone woke up, or when I crawled into an empty bed.

I wasn't sure if this sort of pain ever lessened. Sometimes, it'd be a song on the radio or seeing the funnies in the paper that he loved so much which caused me grief, or a flood of memories of days gone by would surface bringing me back to a time when he was still with me. Most days, I pushed through the loss and pain, others, I curled in a ball in my bed and sobbed. Fifty years of marriage to my love, Corny, but it didn't seem long enough.

"Mom, do you mind if I hang out with Mya tonight? Her dad said I could sleep over if it was okay with you." Sophie came into the kitchen and grabbed a bottle of water from the fridge.

"Sure, but I want you home before noon tomorrow. Maude and I have work Monday, and we'll need to go and get groceries for the week."

"Which reminds me, make sure you put anything you want for lunches this week for you and the younger two on the list by the fridge," I said.

"I will." Sophie leaned over to stare at the bacon, inhaling deeply as she did. "This smells so good."

"Ah, hands off until it's done." I swatted. "Now you're acting like Corny, out here trying to steal food before it's finished cooking."

"Can't blame me for trying, everything looks so freaking good." Her stomach growled.

Kerrie and I had a pretty good system going now that they were settled. We rode to work together in the mornings, leaving my car here just in case Sophie had any emergencies or issues. She'd gotten her license a few days ago. We split the chores like dishes, laundry, vacuuming, and cooking, which was nice, as that meant some nights I could sit and relax.

When we finished brunch, Sophie did the dishes, while I went into my room to fold laundry. What would my life be like if I hadn't become friends with Piper and Kerrie? They'd been lifesavers for me.

I stared at the cherry wooden box atop my dresser, the one that housed Corny's ashes. A lump formed in my throat as I walked over and grabbed it, sitting on the edge of my bed. Tears slid down my cheeks.

God, how I missed him. I missed his smile, his laugh, the way his eyes twinkled when he teased me. I missed the way he smacked his lips during meals, and our drives into work. Most of all, I missed hearing the words, 'I love you.'

"Soon, Corny, I'll be ready to deal with things and give you the proper sendoff you deserve. I hope you can see me from where you are and know I'm doing okay. Kerrie and the kids have brightened my life so much. Not to mention Piper and Carlos. They'll never replace you, but they're a nice distraction."

I rubbed my hand across the box, my wedding band glinting in the light that shone through my bedroom window.

"I love you, old man. Someday, we'll be together again. Not quite yet, though. I have a lot more to do here, it seems. Kerrie and the kids need me. And Piper will need a lot of support, too, as she tries to figure out her own life. Who would've thought *All For You Greeting Cards* would give me a surrogate family?"

A knock sounded on my door, and I got up to put Corny's ashes back on my dresser for now.

"Grandma Maude?" Sophie called from outside my room.

"Be right there." I wiped the wetness from my eyes and hurried to the door to open it. "Did you need something?"

She flushed. "I actually wondered if you'd be okay with me driving your car over to Mya's? She has to work early tomorrow, so I didn't want to bother her for a ride home if I didn't have to."

I smiled. "Sure. Let me get the keys."

We went to the dining room and grabbed them from a hook hanging on the wall.

"Thank you." She leaned over and gave me a big hug.

"Remember, put your seatbelt on and no phone or texting or any of that garbage while you're driving," I said.

"I promise!" She raised her hand in a sort of pledge.

"Tell Demarcus I said hi," Kerrie called from where she had settled onto the floor to play cars with Tommy.

Sophie rolled her eyes. "I will, but you could call him, you know."

Kerrie chuckled and waved her off. "He's working right now. I just meant to tell him hi when he got home from work later."

"I could stay with Tommy and Nella tonight if you wanted to meet up with him for dinner or something," I offered.

She shook her head. "Not tonight. We're supposed to have a Go Fish Card-a-Thon, remember?"

I snorted. "Ah, don't remind me. I'm horrible at Go Fish. Nella always beats me."

Nella giggled. "I'll let you win this time, Grandma Maude, I promise."

"Sure, you say that now, but then *poof*, there go all the matching cards into your pile. Who wants to help Grandma make some cookies for later?"

"Me," both Tommy and Nella hollered, jumping up and hurrying after me into the kitchen.

"Not so fast. What do we do with our toys when we're not playing with them?" I asked.

"Put them away," Tommy said, trudging back to the living room. I heard him toss his cars back into the toybox, then he appeared beside me once more.

"Let's wash our hands, then I think we ought to get you two an apron, so you don't get too messy. What do you think?"

"Yeah, that's a good idea." Nella took a long pink one from me, and Kerrie came to help her tie it around her waist.

I snatched a blue one with the Cubs symbol on it and got it put on Tommy. I had to work at getting it up enough so he wouldn't trip on it. "Alright, I think we're ready to start baking. Let's give everyone some ingredients to get from the cupboards and fridge."

For the next two hours, we worked on making a couple of batches of chocolate chip cookies. Tommy probably had more flour on him than in the bowl, and Nella had definitely eaten a few chocolate chips along the way, or so said the dark brown ring around her mouth.

When they were piping hot, I set one down on each of their plates. "You know what's good with a warm cookie?"

"No," Nella said.

"A scoop of vanilla ice cream." I moved toward the freezer to grab the container of ice cream.

"Grandma Maude sure knows how to spoil you guys," Kerrie said, laughing. "It sounds good, although my hips might disagree."

"Well, you only live once. Might as well enjoy the small things."

That had become my new mantra. Enjoy the small things. Because none of us really knew how much time we had here. I wanted to do everything I could, while I could. Not just for me, but because Corny no longer could. It was my duty to make sure Kerrie, her kids, Piper, Carlos, and I did a lot of fun, memorable things. That way, when it was my time to go, I'd be ready. Although, I'd make sure I was around for a long while yet. I had to see the kids grown and doing well, and Kerrie and Piper happily settled in with their lives.

Yep, there were so many things left to do.

Chapter Twenty-Two

PIPER

Three Months Later...

I sat on my couch with my legs tucked under me, sipping a cup of hot cocoa. Work had been busy due to us trying to get all our last-minute ideas put together for a new line of cards we were going to put out this winter. Mr. Dancy had been really pushing everyone this week like he was a drill sergeant rather than our frugal old boss.

Maude wondered if he had something up his sleeve he wanted us to all be freed up for, which could mean anything at All For You Greeting Cards. As long as it wasn't another "spa weekend," I was sure I'd be fine.

But it wasn't just work I had on my mind. For the last couple of months, I'd really been considering my stepdad's offer to help me find another apartment. Even though I'd only run into Minho a handful of times, I realized now, more than ever, I was ready for a change. Kind of an out with the old, in with the new mentality. With a sigh, I stood and stared through my balcony windows to Lake Michigan. God, I'd miss the view, but it was time to start working on the new and improved Piper. Someone who was stronger, wiser, and hopefully not as apt at getting their heart broken.

Turning, I went over to the kitchen counter and grabbed my cell phone. Okay, it was now or never. I dialed my stepdad's number, hoping he was in town.

"Hey, kiddo," he answered after a few rings. "How are things going?"

"They're going well. Busy, you know, the usual stuff." I laughed, leaning against the wall. "So, I wondered if your offer was still open about helping me find another apartment?"

"Of course. I can get ahold of a few of my building managers to see what we have open, then send you the links with addresses." David paused. "Would you want to go look at them tonight yet or tomorrow?"

"Either or is fine with me." Although, I'd have to put real clothes back on, since I'd slipped into a pair of sweatpants when I'd gotten home earlier.

"Alright, let me call you back once I've made arrangements," he said.

After he hung up, I went into my room and threw on a pair of jeans and a nice sweater. I had no idea what area he'd have me looking at places, but I didn't want to look like a slob.

About twenty minutes later, David called back. "Alright, I've got four lined up for you to go see. They're kind of spread out in various areas, but all within walking distance to your work. I'm out of town right now, otherwise I'd offer to go with you."

"No, that's fine. I can call Maude or Kerrie to see if one of them might want to tag along. Do you know the price range?"

"Let's not worry about that just yet," David said. "If you find one you like or want, I'll work with you on it."

My eyes welled. "You don't have to do that, you know?"

He chuckled. "I know, but you're still my daughter and I want to make sure you've got a nice, safe place to live. I just sent over the links to your phone, so keep me posted on what you think. I let the managers know you'd be around tonight, so stop at the front desks and they'll have keys for you. Well, other than the brownstone. They'll leave the key in the mailbox with a number four on it."

"Perfect, thank you, and I love you, Dad."

"Love you, too. I'll talk to you soon."

Once he let me go again, I decided to call Maude, remembering Kerrie's son was supposed to start karate tonight. Hopefully, Maude could go with me. She was pretty no nonsense, but also observant and could easily point out pros and cons of each of the places.

I brought up her contact information and hit the Call button.

"Hello, this Maude."

"Hey, it's Piper. Are you busy for the next couple of hours?"

"Not really, just sitting at the house watching the boob-tube," she said.

I laughed. "Okay, well, I wondered if you might be able to go look at a few apartments with me?"

"Hot diggity damn, are you really going to finally move?"

"Maybe. I'm weighing my options."

"Just let me get my shoes on and grab my purse. Did you want me to pick you up or did you want meet somewhere?"

Since I'd let Minho keep our vehicle at the time of our breakup, I didn't have one any longer. Not that I normally needed one since I was like two seconds from the various modes of public transportation. Although, maybe next year I'd purchase myself a new car, but I decided to tackle one thing at a time, and first up was an apartment.

"If you could pick me up, I'd appreciate it. I can give you some gas money for running me around," I offered.

"Sounds good. I'll be there shortly," Maude said before letting me go.

I snatched my purse and jacket, then headed down to the main lobby to wait for Maude. While standing there, I scrolled through the listings David had sent me. The first was an old brownstone that'd been converted into apartments. The next was a large apartment building further away from the shoreline, but it had a lot of great amenities like a gym, a parking garage, a restaurant on the lower level, and a rooftop bar. The other two were also away from the shoreline, but with great views of the cityscape.

When Maude pulled up, I rushed to her parked car and slipped into the passenger side. "Hi, thank you for coming on such short notice."

"Ah, that's what friends are for. Besides, you might need a second opinion, and you can't trust just anyone." She smiled, her bright pink lipstick practically glowing. "So, where to first?"

I gave her directions to the apartment furthest away. "This one has some great amenities, so hopefully the apartment itself is nice."

When we got to the building, the one nice thing I could say was it was tall and kind of close to some of the other apartment buildings or offices. We found parking in a side lot, which David had given me the code to get into, so we wouldn't have to pay a fee, which was great.

Maude and I made our way into the lobby, filled with dark marble, a small fountain, and a main desk area.

I made a beeline for the desk, finding a tall blonde lady dressed in a dark suit jacket and matching pants. "Hi, I'm Piper Mishner. I'm here to look at an apartment."

"Hi, and welcome. I have the key right here. It's for room 506 on the fifth floor. You'll take a right out of the elevator. Let me know if you have any questions after you look at it, or would like any other information."

"Thank you, I will." I took the key from her, and Maude and I made our way to the elevators.

"I hate elevators," Maude said when we got inside. "One time, during a storm, Mr. Dancy and I got stuck in one together. You know how slowly time goes by when that man gets to talking about his gout?" She crossed herself as if to ward off evil.

"Well, the good news is, it isn't storming, and I don't have gout." I chuckled, pressing the button for the fifth floor.

We arrived at the right floor, and we headed in the direction of the apartment. I unlocked the door, and we walked into an open area which included a nice sized living room, attached directly to a kitchen that had white granite countertops. There were two stools pushed in under the island. I realized right away there was nowhere to put my dining table.

"Let's open the windows and check out the view." Maude moved to the shades and tugged on the strings to pull them up. She gasped. "Jesus H. Christ. You've got a nice view of the moon from here."

"The moon? It's still light out how can you see…"

Holy shit. There, standing in the window in the apartment complex right across from this one, was a naked man, his ass cheeks pressed against the glass, and a woman right in front of him, doing God only knew what.

"Oh, geez. I can't unsee that."

"Well, I guess you can have dinner and a show after work every night." She let the shades fall back into place with a resounding thud.

"So, I'm guessing I know why the previous tenant moved." My face warmed.

"Do you want to go look at the bedroom?" Maude turned to me, her brows raised.

"I'll have to say no. I think this place is a little too close to the neighbors. And that city view in the photos does not match our view here."

Maude snorted. "Yeah, I doubt anything will match that view. Are we onto the next, then?"

"Most definitely," I said, clutching my purse to my chest as we relocked the room and headed back downstairs.

"I should tell Griff about this place. Maybe he'll move," Maude said from beside me as we drove toward the next listing.

"Eww, I think I just threw up in my mouth." My nose wrinkled.

She laughed at me. "Now you know how I feel."

The brownstone apartment was our next stop. We parked in the narrow driveway, and I went to fish the key out of the mailbox like David had instructed.

"This one is on the fourth floor."

"Hmm, I love these old brownstones. It's kind of sad the majority of them have been turned into multi-units." She peered around, her eyes resting on the flower boxes on the porch.

We went inside, then followed the steep stairs to the top floor. When we opened the door, we found ourselves in a narrow hallway, which led into a kitchen the size of the backseat of Maude's car. The fridge was more of a mini fridge, and the stove looked like someone had taken it out of an RV or something.

"Yikes, this is kind of tiny. Maybe the rest of the house will make up for it." I tried to remain optimistic.

"Well, the good news is you can fit a bed in the bedroom. The bad news is that's all you can fit in there. But you can probably sit on your bed and go through your closet at the same time, so I guess there's that." Maude glanced at me.

"I'm not really feeling this place. For the sheer and simple fact it's as big as a doll house."

"Alright, then let's move onto another one."

Maude led me back outside, and I slipped the key into the mailbox where I'd found it.

The next two apartments weren't bad, but they definitely didn't feel like home to me. Not that I was being picky, but I wanted to love the place I lived in. Kind of like I did now. When we arrived back at my place, we sat in Maude's car for a few minutes.

"Thanks for coming along tonight. I appreciate it."

"No problem. It was good to get out for a bit. Don't get down about not finding something yet, the right place will come along." She patted my arm before I climbed from her vehicle.

"I know. Oh, and before I forget, here's some money for gas." I slipped some bills from my purse to give to her.

"Nah, don't worry about it. We got a good show out of this trip. Consider me paid in full." She laughed, waving me off.

"Are you sure?"

"Positive. See you tomorrow at work."

I watched her pull away and headed toward my building.

Right then, my phone went off. David had sent me one last listing, with a message that said, *This might be more to your liking.*

Shoot. I could call Maude to come back, but I didn't want her to have to be out driving after dark, which I knew she hated. So instead, I called a cab, and headed toward the next apartment.

I was surprised to find it nestled near Navy Pier. This was an expensive area. Taking a deep breath, I ambled into the tall building, which boasted lots of windows. The lobby was gorgeous, done in white marbles and beautiful dark leather furniture. Large chandeliers made of anchors, rope, and crystal hung from the ceilings.

Gripping tight to my purse strap, I went to get the key from the receptionist and headed up to the eighth floor. Hopefully, the elevators never went out as I'd hate to trudge up that many flights of stairs.

When I got to the right floor, I followed the shiny white tiles to a large door. As soon as it swung open, I knew this apartment was the one I wanted. My gaze immediately went to the floor to ceiling windows overlooking both Navy Pier and the Riverwalk.

"Oh, my." I hurried over the dark hardwood, past a kitchen with gray granite countertops and shiny blue and white tile backsplash. The living room was huge, and had a balcony that expanded the whole length of the room. A fireplace made of river rock was nestled against one of the side walls, a mantel of solid cherry above it.

This was it. What I'd been looking for. Even now, I felt at ease as I moved onto the deck overlooking Lake Michigan. Boats were anchored in the distance, bobbing up and down.

I could imagine myself sitting out here in the mornings with a cup of coffee. I looked around me, and it was nice to find no other balconies next to mine. There were some further up, but nothing too close. And, most importantly, none of those decks would have Minho sitting on them.

Finally, I'd be able to move on.

Chapter Twenty-Three

KERRIE

I sat in my office after a meeting with the marketing team. Our new line of cards was going to launch in November, and the early number predictions were looking good. A smile curved my lips. We'd been working so hard the last couple of months to get this ready.

Mr. Dancy poked his head in my office, reminding me of turtle peering out from its shell. "Kerrie, I need to meet with you for a few minutes."

My mouth went dry. Oh God, had he finally decided to fire me? The stint jail was a while ago now, but maybe he'd been waiting for the right moment to let me go. Wringing my hands together, I stood.

"Sure. Should I bring anything with me?" *Like pack up my desk? My purse?*

"No, just want to talk." He led me down the hall and into his office. "Go ahead and have a seat."

I did as he said, my gaze searching his face for some sort of clue as to what this meeting was about. Had I used too many salt packets? Did I clock in too early? Crap, I wish he'd get on with it. My brow furrowed.

"You might be wondering why I called you in here." He leaned back in his chair, nearly falling out of it. But he caught himself and readjusted as if nothing had happened.

I wet my lips. "Yes, the thought crossed my mind."

He chuckled. "Don't look so scared, I'm not going to attack you. In fact, I wanted to talk to you about a promotion."

Wait, what did he just say?

"A promotion?" I repeated his words as if in disbelief.

"Yes. To be honest with you, my wife's been sick these past couple of months, and I'm thinking about taking some time off. But in order to do that, I need someone trustworthy to step up and run things for a bit. Someone with a good mind in regard to sales and such. Someone like you."

"I, um, I'm not sure what to say. I haven't really been here as long as some of the others."

He waved me off like he was swatting a fly. "You are great with numbers, and you get along with everyone. You come to your meetings prepared. I'd like it if you could step into the new position I'm creating. Vice President of All For You Greeting Cards. Of course, I'd still be in charge, but I'd leave a lot of the day-to-day decisions to you. Also, Maude will assist you. I was going to offer her the job, but she said she's too old, and not that I'm age discriminating, but I'd prefer to have someone on board who isn't thinking of retiring in the next few years."

"Are you sure?" I asked, waiting for the punchline. Maybe Mr. Dancy had lost his mind. It definitely wouldn't be the first time.

"Very. So, what do you say? You can try it out in the interim if you'd like, see how things go. Eventually, I'd like to hand over all the operations of the company to my son with you as his assistant, but I don't think he's ready just yet. He's got too many pokers in the fire."

"Of course, I'll help in whatever way I can." This meant I could put more money away, maybe help Sophie with college, and eventually get a place of our own. Although, right now, it made sense to stay with Maude but, at some point, she might want her house back to herself again.

He slapped his desk, causing a loud thud to reverberate, and I jumped. "Great! I'll start having you shadow me this week and part of next. However, the one thing I want you to know is that you can't play favorites. You've got to treat everyone the same, even Piper and Maude. If they're misbehaving, you need to reel them in. And you need to make sure everyone adheres to the policy on keeping lights off when they're not in their offices, as well as making sure the heat is kept at sixty-five, and that no one is wasting supplies in the cafeteria. Money doesn't grow on trees, or if it did, I'd have them planted all over the lobby." He laughed to himself as if he'd just told the funniest joke.

I had to keep from rolling my eyes. Leave it to Mr. Dancy to include *that* in my training. "You can count on me, Mr. Dancy."

After he went over several things with me, he excused me for lunch.

"Hey, where did you disappear to?" Piper asked, sipping an iced tea at a table in the cafeteria.

"You're not going to believe this," I said, hands still trembling from the news. "Mr. Dancy is promoting me."

"What? That's awesome!"

"Although, I feel like Maude might've pulled a few strings." I glanced at her as she took a seat with us.

"I didn't pull any strings, I promise. But when Mr. Cheap Pants asked me who in the office I felt might make a great VP, I said your name. And trust me, if that man didn't agree, he wouldn't have offered you the job. Which leads me to ask, did you accept?"

"I...yes, I did. I'm still in shock. I thought he was going to fire me." I spread my sandwich and cottage cheese out in front of me.

"Girl, if Mr. Dancy let us stay here after he found out about our night in the slammer, there's no way he'd ever fire us." Piper grinned. "Wow, I can't believe it. Can I call you Madame Vice President?"

"No." I groaned. "Also, he told me I can't play favorites with you guys."

Maude snorted. "Of course, he'd say that. But don't you worry, Piper and I won't take advantage of your position, unless it's to get some new food items added to the cafeteria menu."

"Or salt and pepper that hasn't been stolen from other restaurants by Mr. Dancy," Piper added.

I laughed. "I love you guys, seriously. Cheers. I can't wait to tell Sophie. She'll be so happy." And I hoped, proud, too.

Things were finally starting to look up. I never imagined myself being given this opportunity after Hal had asked for a divorce. Whether

Maude truly had urged Mr. Dancy or not, the position was mine to either soar with or fail at.

Either way, I looked forward to the challenge.

Chapter Twenty-Four

MAUDE

I sat in my rocking chair, blowing the steam from my cup of coffee while reaching for another shortbread cookie. Kerrie had taken Tommy to karate practice, and Nella had tagged along so she could play with one of her friends who'd also be there.

Sophie came into the living room, peering at me, her hands clasped in front of her. She glanced around almost nervously.

"You have something you want to say?" I asked, getting straight to the point. No sense in making us both uncomfortable with her fidgeting.

"Yeah, I wondered if I could talk to you about some things. I'm not real sure how to broach the subject with Mom."

I set my cup down. "Are you needing the birds and bees talk or whatever it is you kids call it nowadays?"

"Um, definitely not." She laughed. "I've already had that one." Sophie moved toward the couch and plopped on it, grabbing a throw pillow to clutch in her lap.

"Phew, that'll make this talk a lot easier," I said, letting out a breath of relief. "What's on your mind, kid?"

"So, with the help of Carlos and my art teacher, I've put together a portfolio to an art school in New York. I sent everything out yesterday. The thing is, I'm nervous about telling Mom. I know she depends on me a lot, and, I just don't want to hurt her or make her worry, or anything like that."

"Oh, I see."

"Yeah, but what's even worse, I haven't even told Mya yet, either. She wanted us to go to the same college, but I realized after working with Carlos this summer how much I love art and want to pursue that." She sighed, running her hands over the throw pillow. "I feel like I'm going to upset everyone with my decision, but I know this is what I'm passionate about."

"Sophie, you need to pursue *your* dreams. Trust me when I say, your mom is strong, and she'll be okay. Look at how far she's come since the divorce. She's out here kicking butt and taking names. Going from being a stay-at-home mom to the new VP of All For You Greeting Cards. And she's raised some amazing kids, if I do say so myself."

"I know, I'm proud of her. She's always put us kids first."

"Exactly. She'll understand, and the sooner you tell her, the sooner she'll be able to get used to the idea of you being in New York. You should also come clean with Mya, too. Don't wait too long to tell her. She'll be more hurt if you keep it from her."

Sophie smiled, her eyes welling. "You're right, of course."

"Damn right, I am, but I also have decades of experience. These wrinkles were earned like merit badges, kid," I rubbed my old hands together.

"I don't know why I was freaking out so much. It's just, I don't want to let anyone down, you know?"

"Trust me, Sophie, you won't be letting anyone down. Your mom, when she finds out, will be so proud of you. She knows you're going to make your own choices as you mature, and this is one of them."

"I don't even know if I'll get into the school."

"Pfft, none of that negative talk from you. They have to let you in, and if they don't, they're certified boobs."

Sophie laughed, then stood and came over to give me a hug. "Thank you, Grandma Maude. You always say the right things at the right time."

I hugged her tight. "Anytime you need me, I'm right here."

As she walked out of the room, I smiled. Sophie was strong like her mama. I had every faith she'd get into the art school. She was so talented. And Kerrie would be just fine. She'd proved as much after all she'd gone through this past year. Plus, she'd have a lot more on her plate to keep her busy in the coming months with her helping Mr. Dancy run things.

So many things were changing, but I knew they were for the better. Grabbing my cup of coffee once more, I settled back in, looking forward to whatever the future brought us all.

Chapter Twenty-Five
PIPER

I took the last hot roller from Sophie's hair while Carlos's friend, Juan, finished her makeup. Kerrie had asked us to come help Sophie and Mya get ready for homecoming, and of course, we couldn't say no.

"Is she ready yet?" I heard Maude say outside the bathroom door.

"Almost." I turned to Sophie. "You look beautiful."

Her long dark hair hung in waves down the middle of her back. She wore a short, light blue strapless dress with silver heels. Carlos had done some temporary henna tattoos on her arms that was art in itself.

"Oh, girl, the boys will be drooling over you." Juan stood back to admire her flawless makeup.

"Sophie is not going to the dance to impress boys," Carlos said with a frown. "Our girl is going tonight to have fun with friends."

Sophie rolled her eyes. "Well, you're both right. I'm definitely not making getting a guy's attention my main goal for the night, but if someone happens to notice me and wants to dance..."

Carlos chuckled. "Alright, darling, let's go show you off to your mom and Maude. They're armed with cameras and ready to make you pose."

"Let me know when you want me to open the door," I said.

Carlos counted to three, and I swung the bathroom door open.

Kerrie teared up. "Oh, my gosh, my baby looks so grown up." She took Sophie's face in her hands, admiring her.

"Mom, I love you, but you're going to mess up my makeup." Sophie laughed, stepping back.

Maude began to give orders on posing in front of the fireplace. Some pictures had Kerrie in them, others had Mya, then we made Carlos take a few with Maude, Kerrie, Sophie, and I. Then, of course, Carlos and Juan wanted some. About twenty minutes and two thousand pictures later, Sophie waved us off.

"Okay, I think we've got enough. If I don't leave now, I'll be late."

Maude handed her the keys to her car. "Be safe tonight. Same rules about phones."

"And you need to call me when you reach Mya's house. Her dad already knows you have a midnight curfew, so be on time." Kerrie gave her one last hug.

Once she left, we cleaned up the makeup, hair things, and jewelry still left on the bathroom counter.

We sat in the living room while Kerrie called the younger kids to tell them goodnight. They were staying with her ex's parents for the night since they hadn't gotten to see them in a few weeks.

Maude appeared holding a bottle of blackberry wine. "I think we made a great team tonight. Sophie seemed so happy."

"I agree." Kerrie smiled. "You guys were awesome to come over and make her last homecoming dance special for her."

"She deserves it. You all do," I said. I accepted a small glass of wine. After we all had some in our cups, we clinked them together. "So, I wanted to tell you guys something."

Maude quirked an eyebrow. "Hmm? Now you've got me worried since you waited for us all to have a drink in us to say something."

I chuckled. "Funny, but actually, I decided I'm over Minho now. The last few nights, I've been working with Carlos to design a greeting card."

"And not just any greeting card." Carlos smirked.

Leaning down, I reached into my purse, which sat beside the coffee table. "I've designed a greeting card for my ex."

Kerrie practically spit her wine, then thumped her chest as if choking. "Wait, you mean like your drunk, butt-dialing card?"

"No. I decided to be more mature about things. It's a congratulations on your upcoming wedding card. I did the writing, and Carlos designed the floral art for it."

"You're really going to leave him a card?" Kerrie asked.

"Yeah. In the end, I realized I needed to forgive, forget, and move on. The more I hold onto things, the less likely I'll be able to let go. And I'm more than ready to let go," I said. "Also, I started moving this past week."

"Jesus H. Christ, why are we just now finding this out?" Maude set her cup down. "I thought you didn't find any apartments you liked when we did walk-throughs."

I flushed. "Actually, David got ahold of me right after you left about another apartment opening up. And I didn't tell you all right away because I needed to work through some of this on my own."

"How far is it from where you are now?" Carlos asked.

"Not too far. In fact, Maude and Kerrie have been there before." I tried to keep from grinning.

"We have?" Maude gave me one of her what-are-you-talking-about looks.

"Yeah, the night Wooyoung bonded us from jail."

"Oh." Kerrie's eyes widened. "So, you've moved into his apartment complex?"

"God, no." I laughed. "I was totally kidding. I would never put anyone through what I've gone through with Minho. I actually found a cute apartment overlooking Navy Pier and the River Walk."

"Geesh, you about gave me a heart attack." Maude's furrowed brow relaxed.

"Sorry, I couldn't help myself."

"Navy Pier, that'll definitely be a better view than the moonlit apartment we toured." Maude leaned forward to set her cup back on the coffee table.

"You're not lying." I glanced between my friends. "Also, I've decided it's definitely time I let Wooyoung know how I really feel. If it doesn't work, then it doesn't work. However, I'll regret it if I don't at least try."

"She's right. Piper either needs to have closure, or a new beginning." Carlos patted my arm.

"So, what's this card for Minho say?" Kerrie asked.

"Here, you can read it." I handed it to her, and Maude leaned over.

"With your future looming bright, and many years ahead, I wish you the best of luck and only happiness to tread. May your days as husband and wife be long and sweet, and may you be met with sunshine and warmth each time you meet. Congratulations to the bride and groom, here's to making good memories that always loom," Kerrie read it aloud. "Not bad."

"Thanks. Not the best thing I wrote, but it came from the heart." I shrugged.

"And this will bring you closure?" Maude watched me closely.

"Yeah. I'm ready to be over Minho."

"Good girl. If you need us, you know we're here." Kerrie hugged me. "When are you dropping it off?"

"First thing in the morning, right after I get my last box loaded into David's truck." It was definitely time, and no matter what happened from here, like Carlos said, I need to have closure.

After I left Maude's, I headed back to my apartment across from Lake Michigan for one final time. I'd miss the view and the serenity. I'd waited for so long to find a place like this. However, I knew my new apartment would be nice, too. It'd be different, but a change I needed.

First thing I did the next morning was grab my final few things and locked the door. I ambled to Minho's door and slid the card beneath it. I'd added a small, personalized note, letting him know I was sincere in my wishes and ready to move on. I hoped maybe in the future to mend our friendship, but I would need more time for that step.

The trip to my new home took only scant minutes. I lugged my boxes into the lobby, and rode the elevator up. After I finished getting my stuff situated, I planned on making a trip to Wooyoung's apartment. Hopefully, I could sneak in with someone else entering since otherwise I'd need a code.

Yeah, I hadn't really thought this part through.

Once I unpacked, I took a quick shower, put on some clean clothes, dropped David's truck back off to him, then made my way over to the café where Wooyoung used to get my drinks from.

The barista who'd waited on us the day Wooyoung and I had gone there together peered up when I walked in the door.

"Hi," I said shyly. "So, a man used to come in here and buy me drinks all the time. I was known as caramel mocha latte girl."

Her eyes brightened. "Yes, I remember. He hasn't been in here as much lately."

I nodded. "I wondered if you could tell me what drink he used to order for himself?"

"Hmm, let me think. He normally got your drink and a vanilla chai tea." She smiled.

"Can I get a medium vanilla chai tea, then?" I took out my credit card.

"Of course, anything else?"

"No, I think that'll be it."

I paid for the drink, then hurried to his apartment complex, walking in with a man wearing a business suit as if I belonged there. Once I took the short elevator up, I stood in the hallway outside his place, debating whether or not I should knock or if he'd be out soon. Damn it, maybe

I should've planned this for Monday when I knew he'd have to leave for work.

Before I freaked out any further, the door opened and Wooyoung stepped out, sporting a pair of jeans and gray sweater.

"Oh, Piper, hi. What are you doing here?" He glanced around as if trying to figure out who let me in.

I handed him the chai tea. "Our relationship shouldn't be one sided."

He stared at the cup, then took a sip. His eyes widened. "How did you know I liked vanilla chai tea?"

"You're not the only one who can do some detective work." I smiled. "And, to answer your first question, I kind of snuck in with one of the tenants. They definitely need better security."

He chuckled. "Of course, you did. And yeah, I should definitely have a talk with building manager about this."

"I hope I'm not too late." Taking a deep breath, I stepped closer to him. "Wooyoung, I'm sorry. You were right about everything. About my not being able to let go of Minho, about harboring anger, and not giving you a proper chance. But, I see you now." I touched his face, my fingers tracing his jawline. "I more than see you—I-I love you. Please forg—"

Wooyoung's lips met mine. The taste of tea clung to his mouth as he kissed me. My insides danced like cloggers on a wooden stage.

Yes. This is what I'd been waiting for. Wooyoung.

He pulled back, staring down at me. "I've missed you."

"Really?" I grinned. "I thought you'd appreciate not getting calls in the middle of the night for bond money or being roped into being my getaway ride."

He chuckled, stroking my cheek. "My life was definitely boring without you. And you're not the only one who should be apologizing. I should've come clean sooner about Minho and Hani. It was wrong for me to keep what I knew a secret."

"It's in the past now. I want to focus more on the future."

"I like that sound of that," he whispered as he leaned in for another kiss.

It was hard to believe this all started with a couple of exes, a few nights out with friends, and a barroom brawl. I wasn't sure what would happen next, but like any good story, I couldn't wait to turn the page and get to the next chapter.

Chapter Twenty-Six

KERRIE

"You're looking super happy this morning," Sophie said as I sat down at the table beside me.

"I am."

"Could it be because of a certain tall, dark, and handsome cop?" My daughter teased.

I covered my face, trying not to smile.

When I didn't answer, she continued. "So, Mya and I were talking about how cool it'd be if we ended up being sisters."

I laughed, dropping my hands. "I think I'll be taking things slow for a bit, kiddo."

"I know, but there is a possibility, you know. We're not giving up hope."

I slid my chair back. "I'll keep you posted. Listen, I have an errand I need to run. Can you keep an eye on Nella and Tommy for me?"

"Sure."

"Thanks, sweetie. I shouldn't be too long."

I tucked an envelope into my purse, grabbed my keys, and headed out to the minivan. I'd taken a page out of Piper's greeting cards for exes book. Even though Hal had been such a thorn in my side, I realized I needed to have a working relationship with him for the sake of the kids.

He'd been in the wrong on so many fronts, but I'd also made some mistakes along the way. Even if we never liked each other again, we still had three beautiful children together. One way or another, we had to communicate.

I listened to soft rock music as I made my way across town. Several times, I contemplated turning back around. However, I needed to have closure, too, just like Piper had talked about. Besides, I was truly ready to move on now. Not just by making amends with Hal, but in every aspect of my life. The kids would always be my main focus, but I also had a new relationship with Demarcus that was going well. He made me feel special and wanted in a way I hadn't in a while. We were taking it slow, for both of us, and having things wrapped up with Hal would allow me to truly concentrate on this connection.

Emotions overcame me when I saw our old house, bringing with it a flood of memories, both good and bad. We'd hosted Christmas get-togethers, birthday parties, and family dinners here. We'd also had each of our kids while living in the house.

At the end of the day, I had to remind myself that Hal and I did love one another once.

I parked in the driveway and climbed from the car. Palms sweaty, I went to the side door. Before I could leave the card, knock, or even run away, the door swung open to reveal Hal with tousled hair, wearing a blue flannel shirt and a pair of jeans.

"Kerrie, hi. What are you doing here?" He watched me with hesitant eyes.

"I, um, well, I had a card I was going to give you."

"It's not my birthday or anything."

"I know." I fumbled inside my purse and took the envelope from it. "Look, I just wanted you to know, I forgive you. The only thing I ask is that you try to be a good dad. The kids miss you and need you. And even if we're not on good terms, it shouldn't determine what kind of relationship you have with Sophie, Nella, and Tommy."

Hal nodded. Emotion flashed across his face as his eyes welled with tears. "I'm sorry, too. I never meant for any of this to happen. I should've been more of an adult about the divorce. Believe it or not, I'm thankful you said something to my family. They needed to know. Once you left, I realized I put you through so much. Having my parents know what was going on actually lifted a burden from my shoulders. I know I'm an asshole, and I have lots to learn about parenting, and now co-parenting, but I promise I'll get my shit together. No more women in and out, at least, not while the kids are here. And speaking of the kids, I'd like to maybe have dinner with them sometime this week."

"They'd like that." Tears welling in my own eyes, I reached forward and gave him a hug. "I'll call you later to let you know a day and time. In the meantime, take care of yourself."

I handed him the 'Good luck with your future' greeting card for my ex. I really did hope he had a brighter future. I'd never wish ill on him. Maybe once upon a time, I would've, but I knew the guy he could be. He just needed to find him again.

As I climbed into the van again, I realized I wouldn't have been able to do this a few months ago. With Maude and Piper at my side, they'd given me courage, friendship, and a new family. We needed one another. Even though it was my divorce that led me to All For You Greeting Cards, I was grateful for the friendships I'd made. One thing was for sure, no matter what happened now, I knew I'd always have people beside me who cared.

Chapter Twenty-Seven

MAUDE

Sophie had left to take the kids to the park a while ago, leaving me home alone in the stillness of the house. I could definitely tell when Kerrie and the kids were gone. It became almost too quiet.

I stood in my room, staring at the wooden box which held Corny's ashes. I took a deep breath. For several days now, I'd been contemplating whether or not I was ready for this. But with the sun shining and a cool autumn breeze blowing, I knew Corny would've approved.

I was no longer angry with him for leaving me. Somewhere over the last few weeks, I'd come to terms with the decision he'd made not to continue his medications. Even if I didn't agree with how everything played out, I accepted it now. Because it was hard to stay mad at someone I'd loved so fiercely for so long.

Taking the box from atop my dresser, I held it close to my chest, then reached down to grab the 'thinking of you card' I'd picked up for him. Piper's idea about giving cards to exes had really stuck with me. Although, I guess Corny wasn't technically my ex, not in the same sense of Kerrie and Piper's exes. However, he was no longer here.

Swallowing past the boulder-sized lump in my throat, I moved slowly into the backyard toward the large maple tree that'd been here long before our house had been built. It was the same tree my husband had proposed to me under. An autumn day filled with the bursting bright colors of yellow, red, and burnt orange leaves. A tree that, later on, I'd brought Corny under to announce I was pregnant with our son. The same tree we grieved under after we received news of our son's death several years later. We'd had picnics here beneath the shady canopy and bonfires at night. All our important decisions seemed to happen under the maple.

It seemed only fitting this be Corny's final resting spot.

"Well, old man, it's finally time to let you go. I'm trying to stay strong and keep plugging along because I know you'd want me to, but damn it if I don't miss you." My voice broke as a sob escaped me. "I promise, love, I'll join you one day. So, wait for me up there, will you?"

With fumbling fingers, I opened the latch on the box, then untied the bag inside. The wind picked up as I slowly let his ashes drop. The breeze carried them around the tree and over the yard.

When the last remnants had sailed away, I shut the box and placed the thinking-of-you card against the tree under a rock. No need to read the words aloud. Corny knew how much I loved him and thought of him.

Right then, I felt a hand on my shoulder, and one around my waist. I turned toward Piper and Kerrie.

"No matter what happens, you'll always have us," Piper said, her eyes shimmering with wetness. "Corny would be so proud of how strong you've been."

I sniffled. "Somedays, I don't feel so strong."

"None of us do, but the important thing is we keep going and picking ourselves up." Kerrie leaned her head against mine as we stood beneath the tree.

"I love you guys," I whispered. "You're like my daughters and friends all rolled into one. Thank you for humoring an old lady these past few months."

"To friendship." Piper gave me another squeeze.

"To friendship," Kerrie and I said in unison.

No matter what came my way from now on, I knew I could draw strength from these women. We'd seen one another through the best and worst of times, and we'd continue to do so.

Sometimes, it wasn't always about the love we had or lost, but about the friendships we made along the way.

CHECK OUT MORE GREAT READS
FROM ROWAN PROSE!

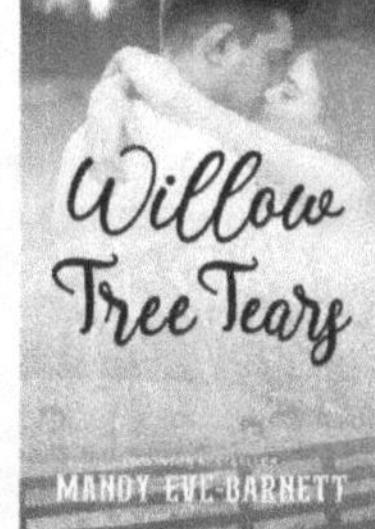

Rebekah L. Purdy is an army veteran, born and raised in Michigan. She works full time for a non-profit as a performance analyst and, in her free time, she writes YA stories across many genres, with more than 15 titles to date. She has a large family, including furbabies. "Greeting Cards for Exes" is her first women's fiction book.